To those who believed in my dream, thank you. To my editors, Frederique, Nathan, and Dad, thank you for your patience and kindness.

They say there's a Demon in the woods, as dark as a shadow and black from head to toe. They say it was once a Dweller, but now is cursed by Darkness.

It pounces when you least expect it and can tear you to shreds with its claws and sharp teeth.

They say there's a Demon in the woods. It has no mercy and shows no fear. Its eyes are a fiery red. They say it was once a child, but the Shadowlands took it for their own.

1

Lady Mary Donahue's head twitched in fear, her eyes carefully scanning the passing trees out of the window on her left. She hated travelling; the old stories always lingering in her mind. Mary and her husband were on their way to the country. They would be staying at her aunt's stately home in Henley, one of the bigger villages on the vast Peregrine Plains, a few days' ride away from the great city of the Dwellings.

She glared at her two guards who sat opposite, their heads lolling with sleep as the cart made its way through Rundlewood Forest. The sound of wheels could be heard trundling through the forest, rickety over the rough, dirt road, which twisted and turned. The wind whistled through the trees and birds flew out of the canopy above into the midday sun, but the horses' hooves hardly made a sound. A branch snapped and a bird squawked through the trees in alarm. Lady Mary couldn't shake the strange feeling in her gut that something was out there; something dangerous.

Goosebumps covered her arms. Was she imagining this feeling?—this feeling that she had become prey. Mary pulled her long, brown plaited hair over her shoulder as she sighed. She'd have to get used to the smell of mud and trees. They'd be staying at her aunt's for at least two weeks. One of the horses kicked at the forest floor and the cart made a sharp lurch. Mary's heart skipped a beat. She had definitely seen something this time. She could *swear* she had seen a figure darting through the trees.

"Woah there, boy!" the coachman called.

Both of the horses whinnied. The carriage lurched to a stop, making Mary's stomach churn. The horses reared up onto their hind legs, the coachman trying to calm them. Mary's guards jolted awake and were instantly alert.

Mary craned her head out of the vehicle, ignoring the thumping of her heart in her ears. A lone figure, clad in black, stood before the horses, a dark hood covering its face. As her guard climbed out of the cart, Mary turned to glance at her husband.

"It's the Demon!" she whispered.

A strangled cry broke the silence and scattered the birds from the treetops. She gasped and stifled a yelp, tears quickly clouding her eyes. Her beating heart was so loud she was sure her husband could hear it. In front of the carriage, Mary could see the black figure whirling about with a short blade in its hand, so fast, it looked like a shadow. Mary's guard was doing his best to get past the Shadow's slashing dagger. The Demon crouched and sliced the guard's thighs, who yelled in pain, but valiantly stayed standing. With the clangour of steel, the Demon pushed the guard towards a tree with brute force and swung a knee up into his groin, which caused him to buckle and fall to the floor. The Demon shot an arrow into the guard's face before Mary could even blink. She didn't manage to stifle her cry this time.

She gazed at her husband, whose eyes were wide and frozen with terror. She was sure, now; the stories were true. There *was* a Demon in the forest, and they were about to face it.

When Mary leaned back out of the window again, the Demon had gone.

"Step out of the cart, Miss," said a female voice from behind her.

Mary turned to see an ornate silver dagger held against her husband's throat, his eyes tightly closed now. Her eyes followed the tip of the blade up to the decorative handle, held by a dirty hand with blackened fingernails. The Demon was dressed in black, covering her arms and legs. Half her face was covered—a black mask with slits for her eyes. The lips and chin looked young.

"Step out of the cart," the Demon said again, pressing the knife to Lord Donahue's throat and drawing a trickle of blood. Mary could swear the Demon's eyes were turning a dark shade of red.

Mary tentatively opened her door, lifted her skirts, and clambered out of the carriage. She found herself praying the mud wouldn't ruin her boots as her husband was roughly dragged out onto the dirt ground. She began to back away into the trees, only to see the coachman still in his driving seat, with an arrow through his chest. The Demon appeared from behind the cart, Mary's husband serving as a shield.

"What do you want?" Lord Donahue said through gritted teeth, his grey hair tousled and messy. "Do you know who I am?" he said, pompously.

"Don't know, don't care," the Demon replied.

Keeping the dagger resting against his throat, the Demon's other hand delved into a sack on her shoulder and emerged holding a rope. It was then that Mary noticed the bow and quiver on the Demon's back. In the blink of an eye, an arrow was nocked and aimed at Mary's chest.

"Tie your hands," the Demon said, throwing two cords of rope towards Mary.

"We are Lord and Lady Donahue!" the large man stammered, while his wife frantically tied rope around his wrists.

The Demon leaned in close to his face and glared into his dark, beady eyes. "Still don't care," it whispered.

Minutes later, the Demon had the pair tightly bound to two trees, rope chafing the skin on their arms. "If you even *think* about calling out for help, you'll find an arrow through your eye. Got it?"

The pair nodded.

Mary sighed in relief. Perhaps the Demon wasn't going to kill them? Perhaps it would be merciful?

The Demon turned to the cart and grinned. This was the best bit, every time. She clambered into the carriage and rummaged through, throwing anything she thought she could into her sack. She found an entire box of jewellery with pearl necklaces and, on the floor, a ring with a small blue stone, which fit nicely on her finger. She gazed at it, feeling a strong sense of déjà vu. Hadn't she seen it somewhere before?

Leaving her victims tied up, the Demon heaved a full sack of goods onto her shoulder and headed into the forest, smiling to herself.

When she was sure the wagon was out of sight, Ebony Wick pulled down her hood and took off her mask, revealing long black hair and pointed features. Her eyes slowly turned a dark shade of purple, reflecting her mood, as she made her way home.

2

It was a warm day above the trees. The dappled sunlight fell through the leaves as Ebony trudged home. Squirrels scampered about, gathering nuts for the coming winter. A fairy darted alongside her, its dragonfly wings shimmering through the patches of sunlight. Fairies were small creatures about the size of an adult's hand. Their human-like bodies were covered in a thin layer of silvery-white hair. They had rounded eyes atop their round heads and their skin colours varied from blue to red, dark brown to silver and gold.

At last, Ebony spotted her home through the trees. It wasn't much, but it always made her smile. It was *hers*, set up the way she liked it.

Ebony lived in a little clearing in the woods next to a large stream. She had been living there for a while now, loath to move on again. With a huff, she put her bag down by the bonfire. Crawling inside her den, a little bivouac made from branches and animal skin, she retrieved a small bag holding two rabbits she had caught earlier that morning and set about roasting them above the fire. A group of fairies sat beside her, dangling their legs over the log, chewing on roots and bickering. Once the rabbits were cooked, she gave small chunks to the fairies beside her, and tore off the rest of the meat for herself. She then put three fingers to her forehead and closed her eyes. The fairies began to make a buzzing sound with their wings and said with Ebony the Fae words of grace:

"I thank the trees, the grass, the leaves. I thank the Mother, the Sister, the Daughter of the Forest."

They then enjoyed their food in peace.

Ebony changed into her green tunic and leggings and stored her dark outfit in the far corner of her den.

She rose early the next morning and rummaged through her loot. Setting traps in the surrounding trees, she set off away from home, towards the Dwellings: 'The greatest city in Atlaan' they called it. Ebony had laughed the first time she'd heard this. She was headed for the market; not the rich Port market in the East Dwellings—the flea market in the Common Dwellings, where she had grown up. Everyone knew it was the best place to sell illegal wares.

The Port market sold everything you could ever need. But the Common market sold so much more than that and it always kept its secrets.

As she left the woodland and entered the slums of the Common Dwellings, Ebony took off the ring she had found the day before. It could sell for quite a bit, but as it shimmered in the sun, the odd feeling of déjà vu returned. Her brows furrowed as she examined it in the light. She tucked it into a pocket on the inside of her old, tattered jacket. She didn't want to sell it just yet.

The centre of the Commons, a large square, was the centre of the market. Market stalls were set up everywhere you could turn. At night, the stalls were closed; they never moved, but their owners did. The market was run by gangs, which was why Ebony preferred to work on the fringes. Donkeys laden with goods trundled by, their owners dragging them along. Urchins weaved their way through the stalls, stealing whatever they could get their hands on and avoiding the Snatchers at all costs. The Common Custodians, better known as the Snatchers, were a police force who would round up stray children and send them to orphanages (known as The Clink); a dark place where orphans and abandoned children were kept. Merchants called out, horses whinnied, voices argued. The market was a cacophony of sound.

She positioned herself in her favourite spot—the entrance to the only road that led back to the port via the North Dwellings—and set up shop on her old wolf-skin rug. Sitting beside her wares, she watched the streets of the Common Dwellings fill up with all kinds of merchants and shoppers, some more discreet than others.

A Southern man wrapped in what looked like a colourful rug pored over Ebony's wares, furtively peering over his shoulder. He would always come to her stall, but he would never say a word, which suited Ebony perfectly; she didn't like to talk much either.

The market was especially busy today because the holiday season was on its way and the bad weather hadn't hit yet. Through the coldest month, people would gather to sing and drink and a bonfire would be lit in the Dwellings Park, which was technically in the West Dwellings, despite the fact that the boundaries of the West Dwellings were mostly on the other side of the river. Commoners weren't often welcome to such festivities.

Ebony often attracted mothers to her stall, babe in arms. They always gave her a pitying look and paid more than they had to. They probably thought she lived on the streets, avoiding the Snatchers. Nobody could know where Ebony *really* lived or she'd be Snatched again. She shivered, remembering the one time she had met their leader, Alastor Bates. One day, she'd get her revenge on him. He would never be able to hurt a child again. She had successfully managed to avoid the Snatchers since she was ten, though she had only been living in the wild for two years. She guessed she was around sixteen now, but she'd never known when her birthday was.

Ebony had never known her family. The matron at her first orphanage had told her she had been delivered there by a man, but the matron never saw him again and didn't know his name. Ebony had given up wondering about her parents years back. Who were they? What were they called? What were they like? Why did they give her up? She had asked herself the same questions ever since she could think. But when she'd moved into the forest, she had decided it was time to put the past behind her. Some questions just had to be left unanswered.

Ebony smiled shyly as a mother bought a necklace and tentatively placed coins into Ebony's hand, careful to avoid touching her grubby fingers.

It was a lucrative day for Ebony, but six hours later, her back had started to ache. The light was falling, and the shoppers were disappearing into their warm homes. She packed up her rug, watching a line of children in chains being led through the streets by two Snatchers. The poor orphans had probably just been caught and were about to meet Bates for the first time. Her stomach churned. Keeping to the shadows, she silently followed behind the group through the streets. One of the children looked to be only a few years old and struggled to keep up. He fell more than once, and the child before him, perhaps around eight years old, helped him onto his feet. One of the Snatchers growled and gave the older boy's head a good thwack.

Leaving her sack on the ground, Ebony glanced up and down the empty street, lined by closed shops. She leapt out from the shadows and drove her dagger under the Snatcher's collar bone. He yelled and fell to the floor with a thump, making the children scream. The second

Snatcher had his truncheon drawn, but he wasn't quick enough. Ebony threw her dagger, which lodged itself in the man's shoulder. With a yell, he lunged at her with his other arm, but missed as she darted sideways, pulled her dagger free, and sliced his throat. He gargled blood, then landed face-first in the dirt. The children stared up at her in horror. She then sliced the first Snatcher's throat for good measure. She searched the two men until she found a small key and began unlocking the chains that held the children together.

"Go. Hide." She snapped at the street urchins, who quickly scattered and disappeared. She stared at the two bodies on the floor, blood pooling around them both, imagining Bates' anger when his guards found them both dead in the streets. She picked up her sack and trudged towards the forest with a satisfied smile on her face.

Autumn was her favourite time of year and trade was good. She was saving up for a warm fur blanket—only a few more loots and she'd be able to afford it. It would take all of her savings, but winter would arrive soon. She could manage the cold sting of winter—Ebony could sleep anywhere—but last year, she had got sick; so sick, she had learned her lesson. She *had to* take better care of herself this winter.

Besides, there was nothing else she wanted with the money. She was content; she could feed herself, she had a roof, she had a clean river, she even had a bottle of rum—what more was there? A nagging voice started a list; *new boots, a warmer jacket, more food, a warm bath …* she shoved the list to the back of her mind.

Winding her way through the trees, she collected her traps as she reached her camp. She had caught three rabbits. She sat staring into the fire as she waited for her stew to boil in the large pot that she had hung over the crackling flames. As darkness invaded the trees, the fire flickered and lit up something she hadn't noticed before.

A footprint. A footprint too large to be her own.

3

Ebony felt a sudden pounding in her chest and the world began to spin. She stood up and went to inspect. It was a human print made by a boot. The foot was large, so its owner must have been tall. She followed the prints around the fire, her stomach in a tight knot. They could be watching her right now; watching her confusion with malice in their eyes. Was there only one of them? There might be others hiding in the trees. Standing at the edge of the clearing, she stood silently, watching.

An owl hooted. A bat flew past. The wind rustled through the leaves, but the forest stood still.

With wary grey eyes, she retreated back to the comfort of her fire and glared into the dark forest. It was no use trying to see anything now. She took a deep breath, trying to calm her nerves, holding her dagger in her hands. The dagger went with her everywhere—without it, she didn't feel safe. It was pure silver and, surrounding two yellow gems, its sheath was embossed with decorative leaves.

When the stew was ready, she found she no longer had the appetite. She muttered the Fae words of grace and ate as much as she could, her eyes darting about the clearing, storing the rest of it inside her den after extinguishing the fire. The heat from the pot would warm up the little room in no time. Her nerves tingling, she lay herself down on the forest floor inside her den and tried to sleep. She'd have to stay vigilant overnight and track the footprints in the morning.

When she awoke, she didn't feel rested at all, her eyes drooping and heavy. She could feel the morning sun shining down through the branches of her shelter. It took her a moment to remember what she had discovered the night before. She was dressed as a shadow again and out of her den in minutes, where a pair of red fairies were inspecting the footprint. Circling the trees around her camp, she checked every trap she had set—the nets, the stake pits, the tripwire, the feather spear traps—but it was all in place, just as she had left it.

Tracking the footprints, she followed them through the trees, her camp slowly disappearing from sight. They twisted and turned in odd directions and suddenly came to an abrupt stop. Ebony looked around in dismay. The tracks had simply vanished. In confusion, she searched the area for any more signs of life, but there was nothing. Either the intruder had literally disappeared on the spot or had suddenly remembered to cover his tracks. Worry and suspicion pulled at Ebony's gut. Still feeling wary, but with a lighter heart, she followed the tracks back to her camp. The intruder would be long gone by now.

Had she really walked this far? She hadn't meant to wander such a long way from the clearing. A shiver went up her spine and she froze, listening to the rustle of leaves and the snap of a twig. Up ahead she saw something moving; something the size of a fully grown man. Her stomach churned. The intruder had returned and lit a fire. He was the first intruder Ebony had ever had. How had he managed to get in? Her traps had always stopped people before.

She pulled up her hood and crept along the forest floor on hands and knees until she got close enough to see her fire and the log she would use to sit on while she cooked. It was now occupied by a tall, bearded man who was fully clad in ragged patchwork clothing. A hood covered his eyes. She crouched behind a small bush to watch. If he dared go near her den, she'd attack. But she'd left all of her weapons inside the bivouac, except the small dagger hidden in her boot. She had been so eager to track the mysterious intruder that she'd left her bow and quiver in plain sight.

The fire crackled and the intruder warmed his fingertips by the flames. He stared off into the woods, his back to Ebony, almost as if he was waiting for something. The woods fell silent.

At last, the intruder stood up, the fire now dancing merrily, and made his way over to the den. Ebony stiffened, ready to attack. The intruder knelt down and peered inside the doorway and, just as Ebony was about to spring out of the bush and attempt to tackle the big man, he stood up straight, pulled down his hood, and turned in her direction with a smile on his face. Ebony couldn't move a muscle. He had a ginger beard, ginger hair in a ponytail, and a strange look of cunning in his eyes.

"I know you're there," he said, sitting down by the fire again.

Ebony jumped and stifled a yelp. Praying he hadn't heard anything, she crept backwards and pulled the little dagger out of her boot. Staying low to the ground, she navigated her way around the clearing, leaving the man staring at the bush she had just been hiding behind.

Minutes later, a knife appeared at the intruder's throat.

"There you are," the big man said, as if he'd lost his friend in a market.

"What do you want?" she whispered into his ear, threatening to pierce his skin with the dagger.

"I wanted to meet the Demon in the woods that they all talk about. But the better question is, what do *you* want?" he said, standing up slowly and calmly.

Ebony spun him around and pressed the dagger to his stomach; a hard stomach with very little fat, but the thin fabric wouldn't be enough protection against the knife. She pulled a coil of rope out of a pocket and led him to the nearest tree. She paused briefly, realising the intruder wasn't resisting her like her prey normally did. In fact, he didn't seem troubled by this turn of events in the slightest. She frowned and pushed a bit harder into his chest with her knife.

"Sit," she commanded and watched him shrug a bag off his shoulders that clunked ominously as it hit the ground. She quickly tied him to a root of the tree and retrieved her bow and quiver, putting her knife back into her boot and drawing an arrow. He was an unusually tall man; muscle-bound but aging. His face was marked with small scars; one above the eyebrow, one just below his lip.

"How did you know where I was?" she growled.

"I've been looking for you, Ebony Wick," the man replied, with a hint of a wry smile in his eyes.

Ebony did her best not to look surprised that he knew her name.

"They're right—" he added. "You do look a bit like a shadow," he said, inspecting her. "My name is Hunter," he said. "I've been tracking you."

Ebony paused and took a deep breath.

"You came yesterday," Ebony stated.

"I did."

Ebony shivered. He had been watching her for who knows how long; watching her every move.

"Why have you been looking for me? How do you know my name? How did you get past my traps? What do you want?" she demanded, the arrow now nearly touching his eye.

"You do ask a lot of questions, don't you! When is it my turn?" He let out a barking laugh.

"Answer me," Ebony snarled through gritted teeth.

"It's a long story—one I'd prefer to share by a warm fire with some rum and stew," he smirked.

"What do you want?" she asked again, through gritted teeth. She aimed the arrow at his forehead.

"Stop pointing that thing at me and maybe I'll tell you." He grinned, showing blackened teeth. Ebony's stomach twisted with irritation.

"I'll stop pointing 'this thing' when you tell me why you're here."

He sighed.

"Fine. I've been watching you work. You're a skilled highwayman; too skilled, in fact."

"Excuse me?" she said, unintentionally lowering her bow.

"Your skills are going to waste. You could be capable of so much more. Looting lords and ladies will get you nowhere."

Goosebumps covered her arms. He had watched her kill the coach driver, he had watched her tie up that rich couple; he'd watched her empty the coach of everything valuable, and yet he had the gall to say she was going to waste? She took a deep breath.

"How did you know I was in the trees just now?" She snapped.

"You followed my prints and left your bow behind. No highwayman goes far without their bow."

Ebony scowled and pressed the arrowhead into his skin.

"I still think your talents are wasted," he continued. "There could be so much more for you working in a team."

"I'm fine here on my own. I don't need a gang."

"Everyone needs a gang."

"*I* don't."

"Well, it's not *really* a gang …"

"It *is* a gang, you just don't want to admit it."

"Fine. I have a gang—but they're not what you think."

"So, what are they then?"

Ebony sat down crossed-legged before him, putting her bow and arrow in her lap, waiting for his response.

"We're bounty hunters. And I want you to join us."

4

Ebony scoffed, then looked into his eyes. His serious expression made her laugh. She had heard of the Bounty Hunters before; a notoriously dangerous and ruthless gang of outlaws. They had some sway over the street gangs Ebony had contended with before moving to the forest.

"What?" he asked in earnest, smiling at her laughter.

Ebony sighed. "I don't work well in gangs. I work alone."

"I'm sure we can work something out. You could even get paid."

Ebony raised her eyebrows in mock disbelief.

"So, what's the catch?" she said.

"There isn't a catch."

"There's always a catch. You want something from me."

"Sharp one, you are."

"So what do you want?"

"I told you already—you're very skilled. So skilled you've managed to survive in the wild alone for two years, I believe? How did you manage that, by the way?"

Ebony shrugged. "Luck. Skill. I don't know."

"Nobody has that much luck."

"Maybe I'm just good at surviving."

"Exactly. You're only sixteen and you're *that good* at surviving. I think my lot could learn a thing or two from you." Hunter grinned at her again, showing his grimy teeth. How was he so sure she was sixteen? Nobody knew how old she was. She'd only ever guessed at her age.

"Why aren't you scared of me?" she asked quietly.

"Why would I be scared of you?" he chuckled.

"Most people are scared of me—they think I'm some kind of Demon."

Hunter smirked. "I know who you are. I know where you live. You're not a mystery to me," he said, then added, "People always fear the unknown."

"You don't find it weird that my eyes change colour?" She gave him a yellow-eyed, curious expression.

Hunter shrugged. "I've seen it before."

Ebony gaped at him, then decided she didn't believe him. She had never met anyone like her.

She stared at her captive for a minute before gagging him with a piece of cloth she had pulled from her trouser pocket. She found a longer rope and strapped him to the tree, making sure they were as tight as she could make them.

"I'll be gone for a few hours. Don't even think about escaping or calling for help. I *will* track you down." She gathered together the supplies she would need for today's loot and left him in the clearing. With a dagger in her belt and her bow and quiver at the ready, Ebony made her way through the trees towards the coach path, straining her ears for the sound of hooves. Fear knotted in her stomach. If her intruder managed to escape, he'd bring his gang to her camp and she'd return to a destroyed home. But she needed the loot for the upcoming season. Winter was on its way and Ebony desperately needed protection from the biting winds at night. She couldn't afford to let one day of work go amiss.

Ignoring the nagging worry in the back of her mind, she took a deep breath and focused on the sounds around her; the flapping of wings, the tweeting of birds, the scurrying of rodents ... nothing more. She moved on through the woods, staying close to the path. This time, she could hear chestnuts falling onto the forest floor, the distant trundle of a carriage ... and, at last, there it was; the soft clap of hooves. As quietly as she could, she followed the echoing sound of the hooves and smiled as it slowly got louder.

Through a gap in the trees ahead, she saw a coach making its way up the winding path. As it came into view, she noticed its dilapidated state. It needed new paint. The horses looked hungry. It was unlikely she'd find anything very valuable in this coach, but she'd give it a go, anyway.

Ebony clapped eyes on the coach driver; a lanky man with short brown hair receding from his forehead. Tusting Hicks, her only friend in the woods. He had seen her, too. With a flick of the three remaining fingers on his left hand, he had told her all she needed to know. She smiled to herself, lowered her hood, and raised her mask to cover her face. She silently drew her bow back, arrow at the ready. Seconds later, she heard the heavy thud of the arrow as it embedded itself into the wood of the coach. The horses whinnied as their driver pulled their reins tight and careered to a halt.

"Who's out there?" he said, smiling at Ebony as she crept out of the bush.

"Driver? What's going on?" said a voice from inside the coach. Ebony froze, mid-step.

Tusting nodded at Ebony and mouthed 'go on'.

"Stop where you are!" Ebony cried. "Stand and deliver!" Tusting loved it when she said that, though it was the most pointless phrase ever, in Ebony's opinion.

"I have nothing to give!" Tusting cried, trying not to sound too practiced.

Ebony nocked an arrow and drew, while walking around the carriage. The man inside had a knife drawn, held loosely in a shaking hand. His eyes were alert and wide with fear. Ebony's arrowhead had speared through the walls of the carriage and stopped unnervingly close to the man's left eye. He dared not blink. His eyes started watering and his vision became blurry.

Wrenching open the carriage door, Ebony said, "Hand over your valuables," trying not to sound bored. She preferred the more active robberies, but she wasn't sure Tusting was quite ready for that yet.

"Drive!" The passenger shouted. "Go!"

"No can do, I'm afraid," Ebony said calmly.

"P-please don't hurt me," the man said, but he was looking over Ebony's shoulder. Her brows furrowed and she took a quick glance behind her. Two gold fairies hovered next to her head, watching the action.

She smirked, and the man saw a mocking sparkle in her eye.

"You're scared of fairies?" she said, incredulously. Fairies were timid creatures; shy and caring. They loved to help her count her coins. Ebony shook her head in confusion.

"Hand over your valuables or you'll get hurt," she said, trying her best to sound menacing for Tusting, who was watching the scene over his shoulder and grinning with excitement.

She could see the man's mind at work. His eyes flickered from her to a large sack by his feet. A bead of sweat dripped down his forehead. At last, he made up his mind and reached for the sack.

"Th-there's nothing in here of worth, except..." he mumbled, extracting a large pouch that jingled. He handed it over to Ebony's outstretched hand, being careful not to touch her.

"And that cuff on your wrist," she said.

"I-it's only iron..."

Ebony shrugged. "I want it."

He fumbled to get it off and handed it to her, a look of confusion in his furrowed brow.

Ebony pulled her arrow out of the wooden coach and stored it in her quiver, leaving the man muttering to himself and Tusting with a happy grin on his face. Once she was hidden from view, Ebony pulled a small, empty pouch out of her pocket and sat down on the forest floor to count her loot. Two fairies instantly joined her, piling it into towers, though the coins were heavy for them to carry.

It wasn't much. She put a quarter of it into the smaller pouch and tucked it into her pocket. It was a small price to pay for Tusting's cooperation. She would give it to him tomorrow when they met at their normal rendezvous place.

She made her way back to camp, much earlier than anticipated, wondering if her prisoner had managed to escape. If he had, she would be in trouble. Her camp may have been looted already, her whereabouts discovered, and the information sold to the Snatchers. She crept towards her camp, fearing traps had been set up for her return.

Through the trees, she saw Hunter sat right where she had left him. A surge of pride filled her chest. She had successfully captured a prisoner for the first time. He had, no doubt, spent the afternoon trying to break free, to no avail. Still wary that it might be a trick, she carefully maneuvered her way through the trees towards her camp, trying her best to look calm and confident. She couldn't let her prisoner see any of her fear now that she had the upper ground.

"Back already?" Hunter said when she removed his gag. "Not a successful loot?"

She paused, deciding how hard on him she should be.

"It was boringly easy, actually," she replied. If she was friendly with him, he might open up about who he was and why he wanted her to join his gang.

"I don't see a bag full of loot …"

She fished the larger bag of money out of a pocket and shook it at him. The jingle echoed slightly.

She turned her back on Hunter and headed towards the fire, but stopped in her tracks when she heard him say, "Ah, your friend, Mr Hicks."

She spun on her heel and glared at him. "How do you know about Tusting?" She couldn't hide her surprise this time.

"I told you, I've been watching you for weeks. And everyone knows about Mr Hicks—a well-known crook." He paused to relish her shocked expression. "But you're on a first-name basis with him! You really *will* be a good asset to our gang."

"I'm not joining your gang!" she almost shouted. "I work alone, can't you see?"

"Except for when Mr Hicks helps you out …"

"He doesn't help me out, I help *him* out. I *could* do it without him, it would just be a bit more violent, and Tusting … well, he's a friend and he doesn't like violence. I don't *need* him. I work alone."

"Of course."

Silence reigned while she set up a campfire and heated up her leftover stew.

Hunter eventually broke the silence.

"If you let me sit by the fire and have some food, I'll tell you more about my gang."

"I don't want to know any more about your gang."

"Yes, you do. Don't deny it. Besides, the more you know, the easier it will be to avoid us."

However much it annoyed her, he was right. Whether he was telling the truth or not, she knew that learning more about this man could help her somehow, in the long run. She sighed and went to untie him. With her knife pushing into his thigh, she sat him on a log and went to sit down opposite him, keeping her bow and quiver close by in case he tried to escape.

The stew was hot enough now to eat. Ebony put three fingers to her forehead and closed her eyes. "I thank the trees, the grass, the leaves. I thank the Mother, the Sister, the Daughter of the Forest."

Hunter looked at her like she had gone mad.

"I'm thanking the woods for my food," she said, as if it was obvious.

"Isn't that a Fae ritual?"

"Yes. So what?"

Hunter tried his best not to laugh. "You're not a Fae, you're a Dweller …"

"I'm neither. But I have no one else to thank."

Hunter gazed at her with curiosity as she handed him a bowl of stew and a chunk of bread, which he ate remarkably fast.

"Haven't had food that good in ages!" he remarked. "Where did you learn to cook like that?"

Ebony thought back to Hannah, the maid in one of The Clinks of her childhood, cooking with her at night and sneaking food to the hungry children in the dormitories.

"None of your concern," Ebony replied.

Hunter raised his eyebrows and smiled.

"So, my gang—it's not a normal gang, and it's not even a gang, really. We call ourselves the Bounty Hunters. Know what a bounty hunter is?"

She gave Hunter a look of exasperation as if to say, 'do I look stupid?', but, instead of continuing, he sat waiting for her reply.

"Bounty Hunters capture people. Their target is normally given to them by Lords and Royals," Ebony said.

"In the traditional sense, yes. But we're slightly different." He paused.

With a sigh, she sarcastically gave him the question he was looking for: "Oh? How so?"

"We hunt for objects as well as people. Sometimes we hunt secrets. We work for anyone with enough cash to pay us, which gets us more hunts than we can handle, and we work as a team. We're not a gang. You don't *have to* join us, you don't *have to* stay, and we don't lord our strength over others. But we *are* stronger than others—and they know it. Stronger than you, out here all on your own. You'll get more money with us," he said, eying up her fraying shoes and her overall grubbiness. "You'll even get your own horse and gear, as much food as you could ever need, new boots, and a warm bath. You could be a *real* highwaywoman, as well as doing missions for us."

"I'm already a *real* highwaywoman!"

"You're a footpad, not a highwaywoman. Highwaymen have horses."

She narrowed her blue eyes, feeling offended. What right did he have to feel superior to her when she was the one who had him captured?

"Look, I've managed to survive on my own since I was ten. I don't need a pack of oiks to help me."

"But we'll give you more than just *survival*. You'll get that warm blanket you've been saving up for." He grinned at her, loving the surprised look on her face. He would never get bored of that look. "You'll get a hut of your own, eventually—if you're good, which you are. And you'll be one of the only women there so all the men will like you. We like a strong woman."

She scowled at him. "I don't care about men liking me."

"That will only make them like you more."

They both fell silent, but Ebony could see a nagging fear growing in Hunter's eyes.

"You know you have a pest problem here, right?" Hunter said.

"What? No, I don't," Ebony said, doing her best to seem distracted. She didn't want him to know that she was listening to his every movement.

"You do. You've got fairies everywhere."

"Fairies aren't pests."

"They were in your den, taking wood from your fire … they're irritating pests."

"Fairies are *not* pests." Ebony glared at Hunter. "So what if they were taking wood? So what if they were in my den? They didn't take anything I *need*—they never do. And they give me free rein of the forest. I don't have to watch out for fairy rings."

Hunter's eyebrows rose but he didn't answer.

"I'll have to tie you up again overnight," Ebony said, pulling him up and walking him back to the tree, the rope still lying on the floor. The light had fallen and a cold wind had started to blow through the trees.

"I'm going to freeze out here. You might as well kill me now," Hunter said, for once sounding serious. She ignored him and proceeded to tie him up, but he stopped her. She whipped her dagger out of her boot and pressed it to his chest. "Ebony ... let me sit by the fire, at least ..."

She paused and scanned the patch of ground around the fire. There didn't seem to be anywhere she could tie him. She tightened his rope round the tree and saw his face fall in acceptance of his cold fate. Fearing she might be making a huge mistake, she went in search of a longer rope and tied one end around her wrist. She tied his hands together with the other end, untied him from the tree, and pushed him to the ground by the fire.

"If you move a muscle, I'll know about it," she said, showing him her end of the rope.

She crept into her bivouac and tried her best to sleep.

The hours crept by. She couldn't remember falling asleep, but she must have eventually, as his movement woke her with a start. He sat up and stretched, wincing at a pain in his back.

"I thought the hard floor would help it a bit," he mumbled as she emerged. "It didn't," he said. His lips were white and he was shivering.

"Ebony," Hunter said.

"Yeah?" Ebony looked at him, expecting another annoying comment.

"Why am I still tied up?"

"Huh?"

"Wake up, Ebony. Why am I still tied up?"

"Because," she said slowly, "you're my captive."

"But why am I still your captive?"

"Because I don't trust you."

"You do realise I'm not going to leave here until you agree to join us." He paused, expecting a snappy reply. Ebony ignored him, focusing on the skinning of a particularly large rabbit. "Untie me, Eb."

"Don't call me Eb," she snapped, her stomach clenching at the memory of an old friend who had died many years ago. Despite the knot in her stomach telling her she was making a mistake, she untied his wrists and watched him rub at them, trying to get feeling back into his hands, which were numb with cold.

"Light a fire," Ebony barked at him. She was exhausted. He did as he was told while Ebony went to collect the mice and rabbits that her traps had caught, then returned to skin them.

"Do you not eat anything else?" he grunted.

"Hmm?" She looked up at him, feeling dazed with lack of sleep. "Yeah, sometimes I buy vegetables in town." She continued skinning a rabbit and hung out the skin to dry above the fire.

Hunter smirked but fell silent. While roasting mouse kebabs, silence reigned. Hunter tried helping a few times, in vain. Ebony slapped his hand away and glared at him.

"You'll burn it if you cook it any longer," Hunter muttered.

"I like it a bit burnt," Ebony snapped.

"Well, I don't," Hunter retorted.

"And who's to say you're getting any?" Ebony smiled wickedly at his face of longing, his nose sniffing at the delicious smell of cooking meat. He looked up at her with imploring eyes.

"If you don't feed me you might as well kill me now. I'll die overnight, anyway. And if you *don't* kill me now, I'll know you're too weak to kill."

Ebony narrowed her orange eyes and gave a low growl. With a huff, she put two skewers of meat into a wooden bowl, carved by her own hands, and thrust it at him. She muttered the Fae words of grace for them both. He smiled politely as he tentatively took a bite. Grimacing, he ignored the taste, his stomach grumbling in frustration.

Leaving some water to slowly boil above the fire, Ebony heaved Hunter to his feet and tied him to the tree again before making them both some hot nettle tea.

She spent the day whittling, making arrows, setting traps, carving wood to sell in town, and riffling through her unsold wares, while Hunter prattled on about the adventures he and his gang had got up to over the years.

"Got to watch out for The Foryx Clan, of course. They'll never get as strong as us, but they're still a bloody nuisance, getting in the way all the time."

"Foryx? Like those big bear creatures in stories?"

"Yep. They think it makes them sound scary, I guess. Now, the reason why you'll fit in so well is, A: because you're a girl and there aren't many female Hunters around. It will give us an advantage when completing missions. B: you're good friends with Mr Hicks; he's always useful. C: you're a good hunter. You're ruthless, but not foolhardy. D: you're a good age for training: not too young, not too old, and, most important of all—"

"I don't care!" Ebony shouted. She had been doing her best to ignore him, but just couldn't do it anymore. She marched over to his tree and pulled a gag out of her pocket, tying it tightly around his head. He gave what must have been a smile and began humming an old folk song that Ebony remembered from her childhood. A young matron, Miss Matilda, had sung it to the dormitory of girls at bedtimes until she had been told off for doing so.

Ebony managed to ignore Hunter well enough by moving further from his tree, but close enough for him to still be in sight.

The next night passed in a similar way, though Hunter's sleep was more fitful. His rope tugged at Ebony's wrist and kept her awake. She wasn't sure if this was a ploy of his or not; keeping her from sleep to make her weak and more vulnerable.

She didn't dare go anywhere the next day so, instead, spent the day discussing hunting skills with Hunter and trying out ideas that he had given her for traps. By lunchtime, his face began to look pallid and sickly. Ebony tried feeding him, but he didn't want to eat much. That night, his sleep was even more erratic. After being pulled awake countless times, Ebony lost her patience.

"Are you doing that on purpose?" she shouted out to him. Hunter mumbled an incomprehensible reply. "Stop moving so much!" Ebony snapped.

"Let m-me sleep in the w-warm, then," Hunter shivered.

The idea *had* occurred to Ebony, but she had considered it too dangerous. He could easily wake up in the night, slit her throat, and be off.

She stumbled out of her shelter, sleeplessness weighing down on her pounding head, and went to inspect Hunter. With only the flickering fire for light, she saw a shrunken man, green with sickness, a layer of sweat shimmering on his face. Going against her every instinct, she helped him onto his feet and allowed him to scramble into her bivouac. It could just about fit the two of them and got stuffy and warm very quickly. But Hunter was still at last and Ebony fell into a deep sleep, waking hours after the sun had risen.

5

Hunter was not in good shape. His face was pale and sheathed in a layer of cold sweat. His eyes looked puffy like he hadn't slept for days. Ebony shivered as a gust of air blew in from outside. It was a cold day out there and a layer of frost covered the ground. Leaving Hunter asleep, she crunched her way through the frosted leaves and lit a fire to keep her hands warm, then changed into the warmest clothes she had: a long-sleeved linen shirt and her tatty jacket. The camp was so quiet. There were no fairies in sight, which was odd. In fact, she couldn't even see any fairies in the trees. It was only now that she realised the fairies had been scarce for days now.

"It's so hot," a voice groaned from inside her bivouac. "Talking hurts," Hunter whispered.

Ebony heaved a sigh of exasperation. How could she go anywhere now with a sick man in her den? She couldn't trust him to stay put, but she also couldn't let him die. Not like this. She heated up a pan of water and placed it inside the den.

"Don't touch this, it's very hot. It will keep you warm while I'm gone."

"Where are you going?" he croaked, a note of worry in his voice.

"I won't be far and I won't be gone long."

Ebony grabbed her bow and arrows, made sure her dagger was safe in her boot, and noisily made her way through the frozen woodland towards her old hunting grounds.

She had moved away from this place a few months ago when she had discovered the clearing by the river. She always made sure to move on eventually. Staying in one place for too long wasn't safe when there were Snatchers hunting for you and outlaws also living in the forest.

The only person she had ever shown her last camping spot to was Tusting Hicks. That was until the

Snatchers had got to him and made him tell them where Ebony was. The Snatchers had their own ways of getting information from people. Hicks didn't want to know where her new camp was; it wasn't safe for either of them. She would never risk meeting him in town again—except in a rare circumstance or if she was in dire need of his help. But she doubted that day would come around any time soon.

They had continued meeting at the same place in the woods every time Ebony looted one of his carriages. She smiled as she approached and saw him waiting, staring into the trees. She approached silently until she was standing directly behind him.

"Hicks," she said, and snickered as he jumped out of his skin.

"Please don't do that to me!" he said with an uneasy laugh.

Ebony beamed and pulled his pouch of money out of her cloak pocket. Something shiny fell out with it and landed in a small pile of leaves. She bent down to fetch the ring she had looted the other day, an odd feeling washing over her. Her eyes narrowed as she looked at the ring, nestled in a small pile of leaves.

"That's unusually lavish for you. Planning to sell it?" Hicks said.

Standing up, she admired the ring on her finger, the sense of déjà vu almost becoming familiar. She smiled. "I think I'm going to keep it." She handed the pouch of coins to Hicks. "It's not much, but your last carriage didn't have much in it."

"Yeah, sorry about that. A last-minute change gave me a boring load. Thanks," he said, taking the pouch from Ebony and tucking it into a hidden pocket inside his jacket.

"So, do you have any more news for me?" Ebony asked.

"News about what?" Tusting replied, nonchalantly staring off into the trees.

"Oh, come on. You know what. I asked you to dig up some dirt on Bates—watch him and stuff." Hicks didn't reply. "So, have you got anything?"

"I can't risk everything for you all the time, Ebony. I have a job I'd like to keep," Tusting snapped.

"You haven't been watching him?"

Tusting shrugged. "Just give up, Ebony. He's too well guarded."

"I *can't* just *give up*! I've seen him whip children for looking at him—and, for some reason, they put *him* in charge of The Clink!" Ebony glared at him. "He can't get away with the things he's done."

"Did he ever do anything to you?"

"Well, not me personally, but—"

"There's nothing you can do about it. You're not strong enough to take Bates down on your own."

"Hicks," Ebony snapped. "You've never seen what it's like in The Clink. I have. I've seen children die of starvation. As long as Bates is in charge, The Clink still stands."

Hicks looked to his feet and shrugged.

"I'd better get going," Ebony said. "I've got an … interesting case back at camp."

"Oh? Do tell," Hicks piped up, desperate to change the topic.

"Can't say much more, for now. I don't want you to be in danger again."

Hicks shrugged. "Fair enough. I was thinking—since we can't meet in the Cloak and Dagger inn anymore—why don't we meet here for a drink?"

Ebony raised her eyebrows. "Sounds good if you can find us something to drink. I'm almost out."

"I'll do my best." Tusting's eyes twinkled as he looked at her; that look that she knew all too well. However much she liked Tusting, that look made her want to retreat. She sighed, knowing that even when she got back to her camp, she wouldn't be alone. She'd still have a sick man to contend with.

"I've got to go," she paused. "See you around, Hicks," she said, then strode away, tucking her blue ring back into her jacket pocket. Tusting always marvelled at how fast she could disappear into the trees.

A few hours later, a red-cheeked face appeared in the doorway of the den. Hunter smiled weakly.

"I thought you weren't coming back. I'm freezing."

"I told you I wouldn't be long, didn't I?"

"You've been gone hours."

"I had to find us something to eat. Here—" she held out a steaming mug. "I just made you this. Sit up and drink it. It won't taste nice, but it will help."

Hunter looked at her suspiciously.

"What is it?"

"It's just tea made from Yarrow Leaves."

"Yarrow…?"

"They'll help. The heat will help your throat."

With trepidation, Hunter took a sip of the tea, but couldn't hide the sigh that escaped him as his body began to warm up.

"You need sleep, Hunter," Ebony said.

"No, I need to go home." Hunter began to rise to his feet, his arms and legs shaking with the strain.

Ebony pushed him back down to the ground with ease.

"You'll die if you walk home now."

"And why do you care? Thought you didn't like me."

"I *don't* like you, but I also don't want to stumble over your corpse in the woods."

Hunter grumbled and lay back down. Ebony covered him with one of her empty sacks, which was usually filled with stolen goods.

"I'm sorry I don't have a warmer blanket."

"Saving up, I know," Hunter grumbled.

Ebony looked at him shivering on the ground and actually felt a pang of pity.

"You're a damn nuisance, you know," she said, before heading out of her den and back to the fire.

"Thanks," she heard Hunter respond with a cough.

Her traps hadn't caught anything overnight, and she was out of food. She offered Hunter a handful of barberries in the morning, but he rejected them, saying he didn't want to eat.

"I'm going to town. There's more tea here that you can warm up if you're cold …"

Hunter didn't respond. Before heading away from her camp, she heated another pan of hot water and left it in the corner of the den. Instantly regretting her decision to leave Hunter alone, she took a last glance and disappeared into the trees.

Before long, she was surrounded by people in the Common Market. She stopped by a shop full of fabrics and bought a cheap, thin pair of gloves. She eyed up the display wall of fur blankets, but turned away, heading back outside into the biting cold.

At the food market, a bustling chaotic huddle of stalls that was set up in one of the dusty squares, she bought a pot of honey, a few fat guinea fowl, and a selection of vegetables. She was just about to leave and head back home when she stopped herself and gritted her teeth. Turning back to the market, she bought an apple and a pear for the first time in four years.

She made sure everything she had bought was safely stowed in her jacket and walked back through the bustling town square.

"Hey!" someone shouted. Ebony turned her head to see a woman dressed in a dark red uniform, with a black trimmed hat and a shiny badge on her left shoulder. She carried a truncheon in her belt and her blonde hair was tied in a tight bun. The woman was a Snatcher, and she was looking directly at Ebony. Ebony began to walk as fast as she could without looking suspicious. She didn't want to assume the Snatcher was after her. She needed to be subtle—make it look like she belonged. Otherwise, she might put herself in danger for no reason. She walked into a thick horde of shoppers who lined the square and did her best to disappear amongst the people. But her old, torn, dirty jacket stuck out like a sore thumb.

"Hey! You!" the Snatcher shouted again, following Ebony into the crowd. "Girl!"

Ebony was sure now; the Snatcher was after her. She pushed her way through the mob, ignoring any cries of irritation. She needed to get to an emptier street. She needed to run. The Snatchers were everywhere, and once they had decided their prey, they almost always caught it. Ebony saw more Snatchers appear from alleyways that joined the square and her heart began to beat rapidly in her chest. She was only sixteen—still too young to be allowed to live alone. She still had two years left until she could get her adult licence.

All children up to the age of sixteen had to carry documents with them to prove they had living guardians, but Ebony had lost hers before leaving for the forest. Any children without the right documents were sent to The Clink.

The female Snatcher was gaining on Ebony. She was the only person behind her now. Ebony's breath started to become frantic as she headed for the corner of the busy square where there appeared to be a thin, dark alleyway—a perfect place to disappear. She couldn't go back to The Clink—not after so many years of freedom. And she would never get the luck she had got before. Her stomach twisted and she reprimanded herself for calling it 'luck'. She had lost her best friend that day.

A hand reached her shoulder and turned her round to face the female Snatcher; a woman with cold, dark eyes.

"Show me your papers," the woman said. In a flash, Ebony smacked the Snatcher's jaw with her fist, sending her sprawling. She turned and sprinted toward the dark alleyway. She could see light at the end of it but didn't know where it led. With a quick glance behind her, which she soon regretted, she ran as fast as she could into the darkness between two tall buildings, four Snatchers hot on her heels. Stale wind whipped through her hair as she ran and leapt over bags of rubbish left in the street. At last, she'd reached the end of the road. With little time to think, she turned right and made her way through a dilapidated housing district of the Common Dwellings.

"Oy! Girl!" A male Snatcher called from behind her. She could hear their feet racing but dared not look back. She took a left turn, then a right turn, doing her best to lose her tail. She was in the North Dwellings now. The Northerners weren't rich, by any means, but the place was nicer than the Commons. The North Commons was known for its beaches, though Ebony had never seen them.

She swore under her breath. A road she had chosen ended with a large, metal gate. With as much momentum as she could muster, she launched herself up and over and sprinted through the Dwellings park. In the middle of the park stood a white gazebo, surrounded by fountains and ponds. In a far corner was a small, dense bit of woodland. The park was muddy and slippery. Ebony squelched her way through a marshy area near a pond and a large willow tree, desperate to find a way out. The Snatchers had unlocked the metal gate and split up, hoping to corner her.

Up ahead, she saw a bridge over the Rundlewood river, which ran through the centre of town, dividing the rich and poor. Two Snatchers were gaining on it faster than she was. She didn't know if she could take on more than one Snatcher at a time, but at this point, she didn't really have a choice. A stitch started to form on her side as she grew closer to the two Snatchers, who were standing by the bridge, looking smug. In seconds, Ebony crouched down and retrieved her dagger from her boot. As she neared the bridge, she could see the Snatchers both had their truncheons at the ready.

Only one hundred yards away now, Ebony flung her dagger at one Snatcher, which caught him square in the chest, and raised her arms to her face, protecting herself from his cudgel, which thwacked at her arms. She managed to twist it out of the Snatcher's grasp and knocked him out with his own weapon. She didn't have enough time to finish the job; the other two Snatchers were still making their way towards her. Fetching her dagger, Ebony raced over the stone bridge, her insides squirming, and took a hard left, heading into another housing district. She didn't belong on the other side of the river.

She knew she was in the East Dwellings, close to the port, but she found herself in a part of town she had never seen before. It was affluent and grand, a stretch of houses that eventually reached the South Dwellings, in which politics and learning took place. Only those from the East, West, or South were permitted access to the Southern schools. Ebony raced her way through clean cobbled streets, right, then left, then right again. Not a person was in sight. A cat scampered under a stationary cart and birds squawked in alarm as Ebony flew past. Glancing over her shoulder, she couldn't see any sign of the Snatchers. They didn't belong in this part of the Dwellings, and neither did Ebony. She slowed to a walk, feeling safer now, though out of place.

She needed to find her way home. She took a gamble and turned right, hoping she was headed toward the West Dwellings, though everyone knew that was not a safe place for a poor girl to be. The West was populated by the richest intellectuals who cared little for the lower classes.

The echo of her footfall rang through the deserted streets. The buildings became larger and more luxurious than Ebony had ever seen. Each luscious garden was closed off with an iron fence and had flowers spilling out from various beds in a multitude of colours. The further South she walked, the richer her surroundings became. The streets shone; statues poured sparkling clean water into ornate ponds; expensive shops and beautiful, grand houses lined the streets. She soon came upon a more populated area where horses and carts trotted through the streets with grandeur.

As inconspicuous as possible, Ebony kept to the shadows and found her way back to Rundlewood river, her heart beating in her chest. She followed the river west until, at last, she glimpsed Rundlewood Forest up ahead; *her* forest. With a racing heart, she hurtled into the trees and breathed a sigh of relief. She checked her jacket pockets and, miraculously, found everything she had bought still in place. Even her blue ring was still where she had left it. She had just narrowly avoided the clutches of Alastor Bates and couldn't risk it again. She didn't just hate Bates; she wanted him dead. Her life would be so much easier with him gone.

Hunter was asleep when she got back. She touched his forehead, which was burning hot. She made another mug of yarrow tea, realising how lucky she had been to escape the Snatchers this time, and began to make a vegetable stew. She would leave the meat for tomorrow, when Hunter had his appetite back.

A while later, she woke Hunter with hot tea, a small bowl of stew, and a cold handkerchief, which she had wetted in the small river. Sitting cross-legged beside him, she held the cloth to his forehead as he sipped at his tea and ignored the stew.

"You have to eat, Hunter. You'll never get better if you don't eat."

He grunted in reply, but at least had a few small bites.

"Always stew," he complained.

"I like stew, and it's easy to cook. So deal with it," Ebony replied with a playful snap.

When he refused to eat another bite, she heated another pan of water, wetted the cloth again, put out the fire, and went to lie next to him.

She didn't sleep at all that night. Hunter tossed and turned for hours and his cough became more persistent. Eventually, she gave up trying to sleep and dedicated the night to keeping Hunter warm and keeping his brow cold with the damp cloth. Throughout the night, Ebony frequently found herself asking why she hadn't just let him die in the cold … but a nagging feeling told her she knew the answer. She could rob people and feel little remorse, but it was against her nature to watch a strong man slowly die of cold, especially when she had the power to stop it happening.

It had nothing to do with his companionship; she was sure of that. In fact, she was so sure that she found herself repeating this fact to herself all night as she tended to him. It wasn't anything personal, it was simply a matter of principle. If he tried to hurt her in any way, she wouldn't think twice about killing him.

Hunter looked a lot better when the sun came up and even accepted a small bowl of porridge topped with sugar, though he was still very weak and his cough had reached his chest. The day passed by slowly. She gathered more barberries, well-known for healing sickness, and added them to hot water, which gave it an odd, bitter taste. She had only caught a grass snake that night, which was supposed to be lucky, not that she believed any of that.

By the evening, Hunter was almost back to himself. He was no longer shaking or sweating, but his sense of humour hadn't yet returned. In fact, Ebony thought he was much improved by his lack of communication. They were sat by the fire as the guinea fowl roasted on sticks.

"I got you something from town," Ebony said, almost feeling shy.

Hunter raised his eyebrows and smiled weakly. "Not more stew, I hope?"

Ebony produced the apples and pears she had bought the day before.

"Fruit?" Hunter's face lit up. "How did you afford that?"

"Loot from the other day."

"I haven't had an apple in …you know, I don't actually remember. I don't think I've ever had a pear."

"Pears are delicious," Ebony smiled. "You can try some if you eat everything I give you," she said, handing him a roasted bird.

Hunter rolled his eyebrows.

"Say the Fae words of grace with me before you eat," Ebony glared at him.

"Yes, Mum," he smirked. But Ebony had a sense that Hunter liked being looked after and scolded like this.

The guinea fowl was delicious. They had one each. Ebony shared the apple and pear equally between them and relished the juice dripping down her chin.

6

Now that Hunter was back to health, Ebony felt no qualms about tying him up again.

"So, what's the plan today, Eb?" Hunter asked, his eyes begging for an adventure. He obviously couldn't handle being cooped up in one place for so long.

Ebony was planning a trip to the furthest side of the woods for a shipment of goods that Tusting had told her would be coming. The cart would be full of expensive silks, shipped from distant lands. She was determined to get her hands on it.

"Why am I still tied up, Eb?" Hunter inquired, interrupting her thoughts. She held up a hand, indicating for him to be quiet for a minute. He ignored her.

"Get these damn ropes off me, Eb—*please*."

"Don't call me Eb," she said, distractedly.

"Untie me, Eb, or I won't stop calling you Eb."

Hunter smiled wickedly. "Look, *you* don't want me to go because you think I'm going to blab about your little camp. I don't *want* to go because I want you to join the Bounty Hunters. So, we're in agreement. I'm not going to go," he paused, waiting for her response, which didn't come. "So … untie me."

Ebony huffed. "I'll untie you if you shut up!"

"Deal."

Ebony sighed and reached across to his outstretched wrist. She *had* tied the rope very tight. He shook his wrists as the rope fell free and smiled, gratefully, rubbing feeling back into his arms.

"So, what's on the agenda today?"

"You're going to stay here and stay quiet. I'm going to hunt," she said, sitting herself beside the fire.

In silence, Ebony drew a map of the forest paths on the ground, then covered it over with her foot.

She gathered up her essentials, put on her black mask, and made to leave camp. Hunter's bag was still sitting by the tree, a layer of frost coating it. He stood up, collected his bag that, again, clunked ominously, and followed.

"Stop following me," Ebony snapped, wading through piles of leaves beneath the trees, Hunter in tow. "Why are you still following me?" She turned to scowl at him.

"I'm going to watch you hunt. Besides, I don't want you running off—I told you, I'm not leaving until you join us."

"And I told *you*, I'm not going to join you," she said, moving aside a thorny branch and smirking as it whipped back into Hunter's face.

"Well then, we're at a stalemate," he laughed. Hunter suddenly stopped and held up his hand, catching Ebony's imminent retort. He had stopped so suddenly

Ebony imagined a fox with its ears pricked, one foot in the air.

"I hear something on the road," he whispered. Ebony stopped to listen, but all she could hear was the wind in the trees. Sure enough, the clip-clopping of hooves emerged through the sounds of the forest. How did he have such good hearing?

"I'm not hunting for *that* cart," she whispered.

He looked at her quizzically.

"What's wrong with this cart?" he hissed.

"Nothing, as far as I can tell, but I'm looking for a specific cart—and its path is about an hour's walk from here. I am *not* going to miss that cart because of you."

He smirked at her.

"Oh, come on, this won't take long. Can't you hear—one of the wheels is already loose. Just give it a large rock to roll over and the cart will come skidding to a stop."

The wheel *did* sound wobbly, come to think of it. Hunter and Ebony searched their surroundings for a rock but had to settle on a pile of branches entwined with bracken that would perfectly twist up the loose wheel.

Estimating the path of the wheel, they waited in the shadows as the cart turned the corner, coming ever closer. With a sudden whinny, the horses reeled and bucked as the cart lost its balance, one wheel facing the wrong direction. Hunter ran out into the road, his hood covering his face, and did his best to calm the horses. In the meantime, Ebony crouched low and quietly reached the large wooden wheel. She gave the wheel one quick tug and it came loose, the cart teetering dangerously. Inside was a group of four men who had clearly been drinking since the early hours. Ebony hid in the shadows as Hunter chatted to the driver.

"I'm so sorry to be jumping out on you like this!" Hunter said with a cheery voice. "I was just walking through the woods and heard your cart's wheel coming loose. I thought I'd stop the cart before anything worse happened. If you get down from your seat up there, we can look at the wheel together."

"Show me your face," the driver said gruffly.

Hunter sighed. He'd have to kill this man, then. He slowly lowered his hood to reveal a good-natured and friendly face, with a twinkle in his eye. The driver soon found himself standing beside that cheerful smile.

The men inside the cart were too drunk to notice the cart had stopped moving. They were guffawing at the way one of them had almost slid out the window when the cart had lurched onto its side.

Ebony crept up behind Hunter and the driver, who were busy inspecting the broken wheel. Before he knew it, the driver felt the sharp cold of a dagger at his throat. His eyes popped with fear. He turned to Hunter, expecting a similar reaction, but his companion had gone. He could hear someone breathing into his left ear and could feel a skinny but strong arm wrapped around his neck.

He heard a yelp from inside the cabin and then a gurgling cry.

Hunter clambered out of the small cart, dragging two heavy men with him. He laid them on the earth as they twitched their last movements onto the cold soil.

"You didn't have to kill them!" a girl's voice said into the driver's ear.

The driver jumped in surprise—a girl?

"Yes, I did. There were four of them and only one of me—and they've all seen my face. Oh, and you'll have to die too," Hunter said, striding up to the driver. Before Ebony could stop him, Hunter's blade had gone through the driver's heart. His body went limp and heavy and Ebony dropped him to the floor, a look of disgust on her face.

"You didn't have to kill them *all*," she said through gritted teeth.

"Not much of a highwaywoman, are you? You can't even kill a man. I thought you were supposed to be a terrifying Demon," Hunter jeered.

"I *can* kill a man," Ebony cried in defiance, walking towards the open door of the cart. "I just choose not to if I don't *have* to," she said over her shoulder, then disappeared inside the cart. There wasn't much to find other than a cask of fine whisky and some guard uniforms.

"I'll have the uniforms if you don't want them," Hunter said and took them out into the sunlight to inspect.

Once they had found all that was worth anything, which wasn't much, they hid the cask of whisky and the uniforms in the roots of a large tree to come back to later and heaved the three bodies into the cart.

We're going to miss my cart now—all for just some uniforms," Ebony snapped.

"Ever ridden a horse bareback?" Hunter said, untying the two steeds who, despite the circumstances, seemed surprisingly calm now that their load had stopped rocking about so much.

"I—I've never ridden a horse," Ebony admitted.

"Never ridden? Well, it's easy to learn. We'll teach you back at camp when you join the Bounty Hunters."

"But I'm not going to join the Bounty Hunters," Ebony retorted.

"Well, it's your loss then. If you join, I'll teach you myself. If not—" Hunter shrugged, "you'll have to remain a lowly footpad."

Ebony gritted her teeth, pretending to ignore him. With trepidation, she let Hunter help her up onto one of the horses, who then pulled himself up onto the second.

"There's a first time for everything," he said, smirking at the nervous look in her eyes, which had turned a shade of grey. "So, where do we need to go for your cart?"

Ebony described the path the cart would take and, minutes later, they set off cross-country through the trees.

The horse swayed from side to side and Ebony held on tight to its neck, her eyes a brilliant red and her body stiff.

"You look ridiculous!" Hunter laughed.

"How the hell do you control this thing?" Ebony's horse followed Hunter through the trees, moving much too fast for her liking. Branches whipped at her face and her hair blew about uncontrollably.

"Hold on with your knees! Lightly hold her mane and steer with your body!" Hunter called back to her.

Ebony took a minute to work out where the horse's mane was located. She grabbed hold of the horse's long hair, which was blowing in the wind, and the horse ground to a halt. She watched as Hunter careered on through the trees.

"Wait! Hunter, wait!" Ebony tried urging the horse forward with her body. "Come on, horse. Move!"

Hunter made his way back to her, laughing.

"Oh, shut up. Just get it to move," Ebony snapped.

Smirking, Hunter showed Ebony how to get the horse moving again and, soon enough, she was racing through the trees.

7

Hunter's horse whipped through the forest. They had looted two carts in one day, which was good going for Ebony, though she was still clinging onto her horse for dear life. She clambered down as soon as she could and stood a little distance away from the towering creatures, ready to go back to camp. Hunter smirked at her as she gave surreptitious glances every time a horse huffed or moved. He began tying their looted sacks of goods to the horses and, soon enough, they were ready to ride back to the camp.

Ebony fetched a bottle of whisky and Hunter's uniforms and walked a small distance away from Hunter and the two horses he led through the trees, refusing to ride again.

"I'm not keeping them," she said indignantly.

"Of course you're not. They're mine."

"Thank the Mother!" Ebony sighed.

"The Mother? Whose mother?" Hunter looked at her quizzically.

"You know—*the* Mother ... of the forest."

Hunter chuckled. "You and your Fae rituals again?" Ebony didn't reply. "I'll look after the horses," Hunter said. "We'll take them to my camp when you decide to join us," he said with a smile.

Ebony ground her teeth together and trudged on, doing her best to ignore him. They navigated their way around Ebony's traps and made their way into the clearing to find the fire still smouldering. After letting them drink from the stream, Hunter tied the two horses to a tree close to the river. Meanwhile, Ebony went through their loot and decided what she'd take into town to sell. She heard a soft clunk on the ground as her blue ring fell out of her pocket. She had almost forgotten it was there.

"What's that?" Hunter asked as she stooped to pick it up.

"Just something I looted the other day."

Hunter came over to inspect. He gasped, then snapped his mouth shut.

Ebony looked at him suspiciously. "What?" she snapped.

"Well, that's a nice ring. You could fetch a lot for that."

"Well, I'm not selling it," she snapped.

"It could buy you that rug you've been saving up for."

Ebony paused. She knew he was right, but there was something about the ring that she couldn't let go of.

"I just don't want to sell it," Ebony said, hurriedly stashing it away again. Hunter shrugged and went to sit by the fire. "You stay here and look after the horses, then. Give me some money and I'll see if I can buy the horses something to eat." Ebony began to heave a sack onto her shoulder.

"I'm sure they'll be fine on their own for a bit. They can reach the river and eat the grass."

Ebony paused. "I—I want you to stay here."

Hunter raised his eyebrows.

"You're going to stay here or I'll tie you up to the tree again," Ebony threatened.

"You can try. Who's to say I didn't *let* you before?"

Ebony actually growled.

"I know you won't kill me because you don't *have* to," Hunter gave his signature smirk and turned his back on Ebony to pat the horses.

"I'm starting to feel it would be the best option," Ebony said with a blank tone of voice, then turned away into the woods, heading for the town. Hunter soon caught her up.

"Why are you so averse to having some company?"

"Because …" Ebony paused, wondering which excuse to give, "because I don't work in a team."

"We're *not* working in a team. You're working, I'm following."

"I prefer to do things alone," she said quickly.

"Except for when you work with Mr Hicks."

"I don't work *with* him—he's just a friend."

"So, you *do* have friends?"

"Just the one."

"And do you see him any other time?"

"Sometimes, in town."

"You're not *that* averse to having company then."

"I don't like people. What's so difficult to understand about that?" she snapped.

"But you do like Hicks."

Ebony sighed with exasperation. "And your point is?"

"Get to know me a bit more and you might find you like *me*, too."

"I've already got to know you enough, thank you very much."

He ignored her retort. "Having me in town with you could be a good thing. I can help you sell the loot—"

"—I don't need help—"

"—and I can show you the best places to sell—"

"—I *know* the best places—"

"—and besides, I want to show you the docks and what we do there."

"I don't care about you or your bloody bounty hunters!" Ebony shouted. They had reached the edge of the forest. She clenched her fists tightly and stoically planted her feet as a feeling of animosity overcame her. "If you have to come with me, you'll keep your mouth shut and let me do things *my way*."

Hunter stopped walking and turned to face her, a kind smile twinkling in his eye, which only angered Ebony more.

"I want to watch how you do things."

Ebony narrowed her orange eyes and trudged on without a word. She felt like she was being examined.

"The Bounty Hunters could get you an *actual* stall in a prime spot," he said when she reached her favourite selling place in the Common Market. She ignored him.

Her day in town wasn't nearly as pleasant as she had hoped. Hunter commented on her every move and started actually talking to her customers. No customer ever came to her stall to chat. She was known for being silent.

"You could get much better wares than these if you worked in a team," he said when she set up her stall.

"See, it's always easier to sell when you're working as a pair," he said every time he sold something.

Hunter even tried to start a conversation with Ebony's frequent, silent Southern customer. The man looked at Hunter like he had done something cruel and shuffled away. He did get *some* people talking—mostly complaining. The Mayor had recently been re-elected. From what Ebony could gather, he sounded exactly the same as every other Mayor the Dwellings had ever had. Old, out of touch with reality, and more interested in money than helping people. Ebony had little interest in politics. She was the lowest of all Commoners; an orphaned child on the run. She wasn't even part of a gang of street urchins anymore. What did it matter who said what, who thought what, who changed what? She'd always be the lowest member in society.

There was also a lot of talk of the coming winter celebrations. In the coldest month of winter, the Eastern Park was host to a large bonfire, surrounded by people singing and drinking. The Commoners could rarely afford the money for the drink and never felt welcome in the Eastern park, so Ebony had never attended the festivities. Instead, the Commoners held barn dances and sang together on street corners. She didn't know how the Southerners celebrated in the winter months. They wouldn't deign to lower themselves to Eastern standards. Maybe they didn't celebrate at all?

Ebony packed up her wares early in a silent rage, hoping Hunter would get bored of her and leave her alone. She sighed as he followed her back through town. Even more annoying was the fact that she had actually sold a record amount with Hunter's help.

"You're in a mood," he stated, as they wound their way toward the trees.

Ebony snapped. "You can't let anyone do things *their* way, can you?"

Walking just behind her, Hunter laughed. "I thought I was quite helpful, actually."

Ebony stopped in her tracks and turned on her heel to face him, her brows furrowed. "I don't need your help. I don't need *anyone's* help. I am fine on my own and I am *not* going to join your damn Bounty Hunters. So, you can leave now."

To Ebony's surprise, Hunter sighed and looked genuinely serious for a minute.

"We could really use someone like you," he said in earnest, looking her straight in the eye.

"I don't care," Ebony snapped back, but instantly regretted saying it. "I work alone."

"Hey!" someone shouted from behind Ebony. She turned to see a female Snatcher staring in their direction; the same Snatcher she had run from only two days before.

The woman made her way towards Ebony and Hunter, a stern look in her eye. "Didn't I see you the other day?" she said to Ebony, who shrugged, doing her best to look as innocent as possible. "Show me your papers," she barked.

Just as Ebony was ready to fight, Hunter stepped forward with a charming smile. "No need to, Madame," he said. "This girl here is from the Peregrine Plains—she's a friend of my family. She is staying with us for a while and we haven't got her papers sorted yet. You know what the License Bureau is like—always snowed under with a huge backlog."

The Snatcher looked at Hunter with an odd expression, while Ebony smiled sweetly at her.

"On your way, then," the Snatcher replied, with suspicion in her eyes. "Get her some nicer clothes," she snapped, then strode away. Ebony and Hunter continued back to the woods and only dared speak once they were in the trees.

"How come you got her to fold so easily?" Ebony asked, baffled.

"How come she knew you?" Hunter asked, ignoring Ebony's question.

Ebony shrugged. "They almost got me yesterday. But I got a few of theirs first and got away without too much trouble," Ebony said as if a Snatcher chase was a regular occurrence for her.

"Why didn't you say anything? You could have been caught."

"I can fight off a few Snatchers. Did so for two years."

"Yes, but you had a gang to protect you back then."

Ebony stopped walking. "How do you know I wasn't roaming the streets alone?"

Hunter stopped, his expression looking like he was searching for words. "I—you're an intelligent girl. You wouldn't be stupid enough to roam the streets alone," he said and seemed satisfied with his answer.

Ebony had a strange feeling he was hiding something, but she let it drop. After all, as a Bounty Hunter, his job was to hide things, keep and sell secrets. She continued walking, Hunter at her heels.

"You didn't answer my question," Ebony said.

"What question?"

"How come that Snatcher folded so easily?"

"Easy. Just tell them a believable lie and off they trot."

Ebony raised her eyebrows. "I'm terrible at lying."

"It's kind of what I do for a living. You'll get better at it when you join us," Hunter grinned. Ebony didn't respond.

Back at camp, Ebony allowed Hunter to help her cook and even shared some of her precious whisky with him.

"This is my favourite time of day—when the sun goes down and the forest goes quiet, and through the trees you can see the stars," Ebony said, lying on the hard ground, staring into the twilight sky.

Ebony could hear Hunter's smile in his reply. "No—the best time of day is early in the morning—so early that no one is awake, only the night animals, and the forest starts to come alive."

Ebony looked at Hunter who was ladling stew into her bowls. She sat up and smiled as he handed her a bowl and feasted hungrily.

8

Ebony awoke early in the morning to find that Hunter had left. In fact, it looked like he had never been there at all. The horses were gone, too, as was her blue ring. Her heart raced and her palms felt clammy. Why did she care so much for one stupid piece of jewellery? But she couldn't let it go. Ebony spent a good hour searching everywhere for it, before accepting that he must have taken it. She angrily followed his footsteps into the trees, but soon lost them. This time, he had covered his tracks. As soon as he had seen that ring, his plan must have changed. He clearly cared more for the ring than he did for Ebony. She gritted her teeth together. How had she let herself begin to trust him? But, for some reason, she wasn't happy to see him go. She couldn't understand why. One part of her brain told her it was because she couldn't trust that he wouldn't raid her camp with his friends. But there was another part telling her that this wasn't the whole truth. The camp was quiet. Too quiet.

Ebony stared into the trees where Hunter's tracks had disappeared to, trying to work out why her stomach had suddenly clenched up like someone had kicked her. She had done something stupid. She shouldn't have let him go. She shouldn't have untied him. The Bounty Hunters were notoriously dangerous. How long would it be until they raided her camp? That's all it was though, right? The fear of being raided. But there was something more—a feeling she couldn't quite put her finger on. She grimaced. She didn't like feelings.

She took a deep breath and set about frying some guinea fowl eggs she had collected, trying her best to ignore the strange feeling that had come over her. She started to notice every move she made—the way she held the pan above the flames, the way she pouted her lips when she was thinking hard, even the beating of her heart. Her limbs felt awkward.

"Stop it!" she said out loud to herself, but the foreign feeling refused to dissipate.

She sat in the silent woodland, watching a squirrel scamper up a tree before realising her eggs were burning. She swore under her breath and ladled her fried eggs into a bowl.

She spent the day dithering, furtively glancing into the trees, convinced a group of masked men would appear out of nowhere. She'd need to go into town eventually, if only to buy some food, but she didn't dare leave her camp unprotected. She knew she'd have to leave the camp eventually, but not now—not just yet.

Three days passed. Animals scampered through her quiet camp and the fairies returned. Birds flew overhead. Ebony sat and waited. What was keeping the Bounty Hunters? Why had Hunter not told anyone about her? Maybe they had been delayed? Every morning she reset the traps surrounding her camp, careful not to lose sight of her den and fire. She wasn't about to let anyone else sneak in unnoticed.

One morning, a young fairy found its way into her den, as they often did, shivering with cold. Ebony had woken up to see two wide eyes staring into her own. She had smiled at the little creature and made a warm nest for it out of dry grass. The fairy had obligingly accepted the temporary home.

"Where's your family, then?" Ebony asked the fairy. It looked up at her sadly. "Have you lost them?" The fairy nodded. "There are a lot of fairies in these trees. I'm sure they'll take care of you." The little thing nestled down in its nest and sighed. They weren't known for saying much. Ebony found a small wooden bowl and poured in some clean water from her flagon. She then added a sprinkle of sugar to it. Fairies claimed to live only by that which grew in the forest, but Ebony had learned about their penchant for sugar years ago. She had obtained a bag on her first loot and kept it to sweeten the nettle tea she sometimes made for herself, though her sugar supply was running out.

When she had left the Dwellings two years ago and made her first woodland camp, she had found a fairy with a broken leg. It had taken her a while to work out exactly what was wrong with the fairy because it wouldn't say a word to her. She had fashioned a tiny cast from twigs and pinecones and took care of the creature, finding it food and water. The poor thing couldn't fly for weeks. She smiled, remembering how dear that fairy had been to her in the weeks just after everything had changed.

She watched the fairy sleeping, curled up almost like a cat. Despite its fidgeting through the night, keeping Ebony awake, she missed the little fairy when it decided to re-join the others. Its straw bed lay empty the next morning and the strange strangled feeling came back to Ebony. She let out an exasperated sigh. She had woken with her back to the entrance of her den and heard the rustling of leaves outside.

"Hunter?" she called, and an even stranger sensation filled her.

Her heart started to beat, and she smiled to herself. She could picture him him and his friends sneaking up to her camp, his smirk plastered onto his face. She found herself imagining his red-brown hair hanging loose, not tied up in a ponytail. She quietly reached for her bow that lay by her right arm and sat up, taking care to make as little noise as possible. She cocked her bow and leapt out of her den.

There in front of her stood a wild boar. It looked up at her in surprise.

Her smile quickly slipped to a frown and her chest felt tight. She suddenly felt very heavy and lowered her bow. The boar kicked up the leaves beneath his trotters and turned to face her. Horns at the ready, it charged.

Ebony yelled in surprise and loosed her arrow as quickly as she could. It wasn't a clean shot. The arrow hit the boar's front leg and it lay whimpering on the ground, looking up at her, imploringly. Ebony had more time to aim now. Her next arrow went straight to the boar's heart and it keeled over. She had never killed a boar before, let alone cooked or eaten one.

It took a minute for Ebony to realise what she had done. She had caught herself a *feast*; the biggest feast she'd had in a *very* long time. She laughed out loud, despite herself, and dragged the boar, with great effort, to the edge of the fire. An hour later, she was satisfied that the meat was prepared, and she began to roast it on a large spit. She wouldn't be able to go far from camp in case an animal stole her meat when she wasn't looking. She killed time by setting traps for smaller animals around the camp and collected edible leaves and shrubs, making a salad.

Using berry juice, Ebony painted a diamond symbol on her chest; a Fae ritual to ward away any dark river spirits. She took a swim, washing her few items of clothing in the cold river, and dried off by the fire.

That evening, she felt like she was fine dining. She had a dandelion salad and the most nourishing meat she had ever tasted. To complement it, she finished off her whisky.

She put the leftover meat in a pot of salt, preparing it for drying, and used some of the bones for a stew. She couldn't remember the last time she had slept so well. By the next day, the fairies had taken the rest of the boar carcass from her camp. They liked to use the bones. She wasn't sure what they used them for and didn't really want to know.

After another two boring days of eating pig meat, Ebony knew it was time to give in. Hunter was not coming back, and neither were any of his men. With a sigh, she came out of her den and stretched, smiling to herself.

She reminded herself of her to-do list and got to it. She reset her traps and then headed into town with a sack of cold, salted meat. She heard the wind whistle through the trees as she left the forest and felt a cold breeze go up her spine. It was time she got back into town and started life up again. Hunter wasn't going to come back, at least, not any time soon—and this was a good thing, she told herself. Yet every time someone passed by her in town, she glimpsed their face and felt a strange sense of disappointment when it wasn't him.

Lugging her heavy sack on her shoulders, she made her way into the first inn she came across, The Cloak and Dagger, hoping to sell her meat. It was time to focus on getting that blanket she had dreamed of. Winter was on its way and the cold would soon set in. There were large piles of dried leaves on the small patch of green outside the inn and children jumping into them with glee. It didn't take long for the Snatchers to arrive and chase the children away.

After trading her meat to the chef from the back door of the inn, she ordered a large glass of whisky from the man behind the bar; a stout, bald man with not very many teeth. He gave her a wink as he passed her a glass and she shivered, trying to avoid his gaze. The pub was warm, but not very full.

Sat at the bar were two burly men, chatting and guffawing over a pint of ale. They eyed up Ebony as she went to sit in a quiet corner but laughed and looked away as she scowled at them.

She couldn't help overhearing what the two men were talking about. "Me Mam saw it. She told me so, and she don't make up stories. A dark shadow with blazing red eyes, she said, banished from the Shadowlands. Quick as anything. She reckons it's a girl."

"Rubbish. Demons aren't boys or girls. Where did she see it?"

"In the forest—that's where it lives."

"I'll believe it when I see it."

"Fair enough. Me Uncle also said he's seen it—but he's stark raving mad. I wouldn't believe a word that comes from 'im."

The two men began discussing the health of his mad uncle, and Ebony tuned out. The rumour of the Demon in the forest did make her laugh a bit, but it was better that they thought she was a Demon, or a shadow, than an orphan girl.

By the door, a boy sat alone. He must have been around Ebony's age. He had brown, floppy hair and his face still held the baby fat of his younger years. He sat gazing out of a window, a hot drink by his side, occasionally scribbling in a notebook. Around his neck was a colourful, stripy scarf. He spied Ebony watching him and gave her a furtive smile. Something about him was oddly familiar. She turned her eyes away and sipped at her drink. She was just imagining things.

She downed the rest of her glass and heaved her sack onto her back, ready to start the day in town. She didn't sell much that day, having a glum look to her countenance, and she traipsed her way back home; back through the breezy woods, leaves crunching under her feet, squirrels desperately trying to find nuts for the winter.

She paused and stood staring into the trees, her camp just in view. A bird cawed and she jumped, coming out of her reverie. Walking towards her home, she could see that her camp had been left absolutely untouched. Hunter was definitely *not* going to come back. She felt her heart sink, then reprimanded herself for being so silly. She had survived this long on her own, so she could *continue* surviving on her own. She'd had a team once, but not for a long time, and she had been fine since. She *would* be fine. She would get by just like she always had.

But something in her had changed. Something in her yearned—for what, she couldn't quite work out. She couldn't ignore the nagging thought at the back of her mind, however much she tried: maybe it *was* time to find a team? She made herself laugh off that last thought. No. She did *not* need other people to survive. But Tusting's words rang in her ears. *You're not strong enough to take Bates down on your own.* She sighed. She did need to see what she was up against. And she wanted her ring back. She stomped back to her camp and began setting a fire.

The next morning, she changed into leather stockings and her thin green tunic that reached her knees. She put her jacket on, brushed her long, black hair, plaited it as neatly as she could, then set off into the woods, determination in her stride. It was time she got her ring back from Hunter and showed who was boss. It was time she hunted the Hunters. Maybe they would be able to help her get to Bates? She only hoped he hadn't already sold her ring for bounty.

She followed the river upstream, further from town. The ground started to become marshy and covered in gorse. The trees were spindly and hung over the water, blocking out the winter sun. The river ran for miles. It would eventually take her out of the Dwellings; something Ebony definitely wasn't ready for.

Glancing through the trees, Ebony stopped in her tracks. She didn't recognise these trees. Should she go back and try looking for the Bounty Hunters again the next day or should she continue on and hope she wasn't lost?

She found herself walking back and forth for quite some time before frustration kicked in. She threw a stone into the river, turned on her heel, and marched off away from the river and into the woodland, doing her best to ignore the dark rain clouds coming her way. The trees felt different here. They felt like strangers. The animals didn't know her here. She walked on until, at last, she spied the road up ahead and heard the distinctive trundling of a cart.

In a moment of recklessness, Ebony untied her plait, ruffled her hair, and lay down in the middle of the road. She closed her eyes and waited.

She felt it before she saw it. A horse reared up right above her and stumbled backwards.

"Hey! Alfred!" a man's voice cried.

The horse huffed and flicked its mane as a man clambered down to inspect what had spooked it.

Ebony lay with her eyes closed, the sound of the man's footsteps coming nearer. She could feel them on the forest path. He knelt down beside her and gave her a nudge. She groaned and slowly opened her eyes.

"Are you okay?" he asked in a voice that was surprisingly high for his stature.

"Would you help me up?" Ebony said, giving a weak smile.

The man smiled and knelt down, ready to help her sit up. In a flash, she had her dagger at his throat.

Hunter would kill him now. But she wasn't Hunter. Maybe that wasn't always a good thing. She pressed the knife closer to his throat. He held a startled expression, his hands in the air.

"W—what do you want?"

"Your horse and everything in your cart." She was surprised at how bored she sounded. She had done all this before, countless times. Rising to her feet, the knife still at his throat, she untied the horse and used the rope to handcuff her captive to a tree.

She climbed into the cart and found bags of leather hides and a map of the Dwellings. Her heart leapt—the leather would go for a lot of money! Her only issue was transporting the whole lot from so far up the path back to her camp deep in the woods. She sat thinking for a minute, then took action.

She climbed out of the cart, untied her captive, had him re-harness the horse to the cart, then gouged a cut into his arm. He yelled in pain and fell to the floor, clutching his blood-soaked arm.

That'll slow him down.

Just as she was about to climb onto the driver's seat, something occurred to her. She didn't have her mask on. Her captive would be able to recognise her. The Snatchers would find out where she was. An underage girl living in the woods working as a highwaywoman: she was too distinctive. She'd be caught in no time. With her heart in a knot and her teeth clenched tight, she cursed Hunter for not being there to do it for her. She strode up to the man, who was now lent against a thick tree, cradling his arm with a worried look on his face.

"What do you want now?" he all but sobbed.

Ebony grimaced and knelt down next to him. "Really sorry, but—" She paused and took a long look at the whimpering man before pulling her reddened dagger out of her boot and slitting the man's throat. The body sat limp and heavy and the eyes glazed over. Grimacing, she carved a circle into the man's chest: a Fae ritual representing the path into the next life. Ebony took a deep breath and then climbed into the driver's seat of the cart. She had learned some of the most basic commands for horses by listening to the drivers she had looted. She instructed the horse to walk slowly into the trees and, using the map of the Dwellings, headed towards Lake Ava. Everyone knew that Ava was Bounty Hunter territory.

When it grew dark, she parked the cart near a tree and tied up the horse, who seemed happy to lie down in the rain, and did her best to warm herself in the cart.

9

Ebony could see life through the trees. She left the horse and cart hidden in the trees and crouched behind a bush, peering at the busy scene beyond. A city of tents and bivouacs, all varying in size, surrounded a large clearing. She watched as men and women mucked out the horses, heaved heavy cases into storage tents, and fetched water from Lake Ava, a picturesque mirror of reflected trees that lay just beyond the small settlement. The Bounty Hunters used its water and foraged its plants, but otherwise left it alone. To Ebony, it was a wasted opportunity. With such a large lake and clearing, she could grow her own food and be completely self-sustained, away from the city. But the Bounty Hunters *relied* on the city.

Men in mismatched armour sparred in the centre of the clearing, kicking up dust. Ebony could hear music coming from one of the tents, but she couldn't work out which. She crept closer to the largest tent, which seemed to be a food hall. She could hear raucous laughter and the thud of flagons on wooden tables.

They had places to sleep, a food hall—which meant they must have cooks—a place to train ... the Bounty Hunters' camp was like a small village. But to survive, they had to live on what the city offered.

How is my existence any better? Ebony thought to herself.

She watched a few men leave the food hall, dressed in patched up clothing. Who patched it up for them? One of them was a tall, lean man, with short black hair, a charming smile, and a twinkle in his eye. Ebony noticed a large ring on his right hand, but he was too far away for her to see any detail.

There weren't many girls, she noted. Did the men cook? Did they wash and fix their clothes? The city people wouldn't like that. They were too stuck in their ways to see that it could be done any differently.

And then she saw him. Hunter came out of one of the larger tents and crossed the large clearing towards the food hall, passing by two men, who were sparring. Ebony could just about see a large round wooden table and a camp bed inside the tent Hunter had come from. She had to start her search somewhere.

Ebony counted six men guarding the perimeter of the camp. She walked slowly, carefully placing each foot and breathing as shallow as she could. She encircled the camp until she stood behind the tent Hunter had walked out of. She could only just about see the guards through the trees. As quietly as she could, she reached the tent and knelt down on the cold, damp forest floor. She lifted up the bottom of the tent and peered through the gap above the ground. Hunter's tent had a lavish wolfskin rug and a large round wooden table in the middle of it. Taking a deep breath, she lay flat on her stomach and wriggled her way into the tent. Dusting herself off, she stood up and glanced around. In one corner was a camp bed laden with pillows and a large, warm blanket. In the dark, she could see a few objects on the tabletop and went to inspect. They were balls of clay—round balls of clay and one ring. Ebony picked it up to inspect. The familiar feeling of déjà vu washed over her again. Sure enough, it was the very same ring he had stolen from her. She pocketed it and gazed around, wondering what else she could filch while she was there.

Why had he left the ring out somewhere so obvious? Hadn't he said himself that it would fetch a good price? She didn't have long to contemplate. From across the yard outside came Hunter's voice. It was drawing closer by the second. She lay back on her stomach and wriggled, but she was stuck. One of the tent pegs had caught her jacket. Hunter's voice was right outside his tent now. With a great deal of effort, she pulled off her jacket and slipped out of the tent. In the dark, she fumbled with the tent peg, struggling to see what it had latched itself onto.

Hunter entered his tent. Ebony peered under the gap and saw that he was joined by a short-haired man wearing a large ring. They peered out into the yard with suspicious glances.

"She's too young, Hunter. She can't join us yet," the short-haired man whispered.

As discreetly as possible, despite her shaking hands, Ebony unhooked the tent peg from one of her jacket buttonholes and silently pulled the jacket back on. She dared not move an inch in case she snapped a twig or rustled some dead leaves. She sat crouched in the clearing, calming her breath.

"She's good, though. She's been at it a while. She just needs a bit more training," Hunter replied. Ebony recognised his voice.

"It will put her in danger," the other voice said, even quieter than before.

"She'll be safer here!" Hunter replied, clearly too loudly, since the other voice shushed him and replied even more quietly still. Ebony had to strain her ears to hear.

"You know she won't be. As soon as they know about her—as soon as they find out … they'll hunt her."

"Then they won't know. We won't tell anyone. We won't *let* anyone find out."

The voices paused. Ebony's heart raced in her chest. Were they talking about her? She was hardly listening anymore.

They were talking about a girl—a *young* girl. Hunter wanted this girl to join them and said she was good—good at what, though? Hadn't he said that she, Ebony, was good at what she did? But what could they possibly know about her that she didn't know already? And what about herself would put her in danger?

Ebony's head began to spin, and she rested a hand behind her to steady herself. She hadn't ever had to ask herself so many questions. She knew who she was, where she came from, and what she had to do to survive. That was all that mattered, right?

They were either talking about a different girl or they thought they knew something about her and they'd got it wrong. A nagging feeling told her they might know something about her that she didn't. She scoffed quietly. There was nothing about her *to* know.

"And her friends aren't exactly inconspicuous. Their ... friendship won't stay hidden for long," Sam replied.

No, they can't have been talking about her, Ebony realised. She didn't *have* any friends.

"Sam," Hunter whispered with confidence in his voice. "I know what I'm doing—"

"What *are* you doing?" said a third voice, speaking at a normal volume. Another man had walked into the tent.

"Oh—Jared, hi," said Sam in a voice that sounded oddly loud. "We were just ... we were just working on one of our missions."

"Right ... Can I help?" Jared replied.

"Private mission, I'm afraid…" said Hunter.

"Fair enough. Any news on the letter that went missing?"

"Nothing. I'm sure it will turn up in the midst of a family drama somewhere. Donahue is busting her gut though—terrified her spouse will find it first. Let's go to the fire," Hunter said, "though I can't stay up long. I've got an early meeting with Alastor Bates tomorrow morning."

Alastor Bates? The leader of the Snatchers? Ebony's inside roiled and leapt at the same time as the three men left Hunter's tent. If Hunter had any information on Bates … she had to have it. She had to find a way to get to Bates and be his downfall. If she would achieve anything in life, she would cause his destruction.

Ebony stood up and quietly stretched her aching legs. With her head full of thoughts, she made her way back to the horse and cart in a daze. She made herself as comfortable as she could in the cart and tried to sleep. She had odd dreams that night. Hunter was back in her camp and trying to tell her something, but she couldn't hear anything he said. She couldn't even hear her own voice.

When she woke, the birds were singing, and the air was crisp under a blue sky. She had woken later than she had intended. She let the horse free of his ropes and abandoned the cart. She wouldn't be needing them anymore. Hunter was about to lead her to Alastor Bates and give her the opportunity she had been dreaming of for years.

Praying she wasn't too late, Ebony made her way around the Bounty Hunter camp and waited behind a tree for Hunter to appear. As the time passed, she grew ever more fidgety. Where was he? Had he left already? Half an hour later, she couldn't bear to wait any longer. She left her hiding place and raced through the trees, hoping to find any sign of Hunter's tracks. He was nowhere to be seen. She eventually reached the Commons and made her way into the busy market, keeping an eye out for his bright, ginger hair.

As she crossed through the fray of the market, she spotted something from across the square that made her double take. Hunter. But was he with a young woman? They weren't walking arm in arm or even talking. Hunter was holding her hand—not holding but grabbing—and pulling her past the market. The girl looked ... scared. Had he already had his meeting with Bates or had that been a cover for what he was really doing? Hunter's brows were furrowed in concentration and he seemed oddly angry about something, though somehow Ebony could tell he wasn't angry at the girl. In a flash, they disappeared into a dark alleyway.

10

Ebony pushed her way past the stalls, keeping an eye on the dark alleyway. When she finally reached it, she glanced around and stared at where Hunter and the girl had just gone. The corridor was so dark, she couldn't see any sign of life. As quietly as she could, she made her way into the darkness, careful not to step too loudly. Soon, she began to hear voices.

"You'll be safe here, I promise." Ebony heard Hunter say through the darkness. She silently followed them as the alleyway became more and more narrow. Ebony came to a point where she couldn't go any further or she'd be seen.

"In this dark alleyway?" a girl's voice replied.

"No, you idiot—I know someone who lives down here. She can keep you safe."

"But I don't want to live down here. It's so dark and dingy."

"Well, you don't have a choice."

"But why? Why can't I go home?" The girl didn't sound particularly bright.

"Just shut up and deal with it. You'll die, otherwise. Well, first you'll be tortured, and then you'll die—nice and slowly. Do you want that?"

The girl didn't reply. Hunter knocked on a door at the very end of the alley and disappeared inside with the girl.

Ebony crept closer to the end of the alleyway towards a red door with damp, peeling paint and glanced through a small round window. Inside were various scantily clad women balancing trays of drinks or walking arm-in-arm with men, most of whom were grossly overweight. Hunter had taken a girl to a brothel for safekeeping. How did that make any sense? She saw Hunter talking to a buxom woman with a large head of hair that somehow balanced on top of her head. The girl stood behind him, looking embarrassed and sheepish. She wasn't a Commoner, but she wasn't well-dressed, either. Perhaps she was from the port?

Hunter turned to the young girl and put his hands on her shoulders, trying to give her a reassuring look. He then started for the door.

Ebony darted back down the alleyway and, as quickly and quietly as she could, made her way back to the square, the sounds of the market returning.

That must have been the girl Hunter had been talking about the day before. Sam must have convinced him to give her extra protection from whatever she was in danger from instead of having her join the Bounty Hunters. But why had Hunter wanted her to join the Bounty Hunters in the first place? She didn't seem like the type to go rogue. She seemed timid and scared—weak. Perhaps she was a really good cook and they needed her for the food hall? But why would Hunter care so much about a cook? Why did he care about protecting her?

Ebony had been standing by the entrance of the dark alley, staring at the chaos of the market, when she heard footsteps behind her. Hunter was on his way back. She couldn't let him see her, and he would definitely recognise her cloak even if he didn't see her face. If he knew she had seen … whatever it was she had just seen … she didn't expect he'd be too happy about it. She turned on her heel and walked at a brisk pace out of the market, very aware that Hunter would likely be headed in the same direction. Almost at a jog, she weaved her way through the shoppers. She glanced behind her and glimpsed Hunter's red hair not far behind. He was moving faster than she was.

The doorbell to a shop on her left opened with a tinkling sound. Ebony dived in and shut the door behind her. She turned to the shop window and watched Hunter walk by in a hurry.

"Thank the Mother!" she mumbled to herself.

"Umm—can I help you?" said a voice.

Ebony turned around to find a skinny, freckled boy behind a counter covered in flowers of all kinds. It was only then that Ebony noticed the overpowering sweet smell. She looked at him with a vacant expression before coming to her senses.

"Oh—no thanks. I was just … never mind. Thank you."

The last time she had seen Hunter, he had been so relaxed—almost annoyingly so. He had laughed a lot and made jokes. But something had changed; something had happened. And something in her gut told her *she* was involved. She had to know what it was before it put her in any danger.

After crossing the bridge over Rundlewood River, Ebony found a road that led to Lake Ava. It was dark by the time she reached the Bounty Hunters' camp. The food hall was full, but candlelight flickered in the tent with the round table. A figure inside the tent walked to the entrance and paused. Through the dark, Ebony could just make out Hunter's face staring out across the clearing.

Without a second thought, she marched out of the trees, her sack still on her back, and cut across the clearing of the Bounty Hunters' camp. It didn't take long for her to be surrounded. Five men in armour circled around her, swords drawn.

"Take me to Hunter," Ebony said to them, with no sign of fear on her face.

The two stockiest men roughly grabbed her arms and pulled her across the clearing of the camp.

"You don't have to be so rough about it. He knows who I am," Ebony snapped, but neither of the men replied. All around her, people were stopping to watch. They were mostly men, but Ebony spotted a few women here and there, though the only light she had came from a large bonfire in the centre of the clearing and a few oil lamps hung up on wooden posts.

She was dragged towards a small wooden cabin on the edge of the clearing and roughly shoved inside. There was just enough space to sit down. She watched as one of the guards padlocked her inside the wooden cage.

"Seriously, this is pointless. He knows who I am. I'm not a threat."

"Orders are orders," the guard barked. He turned away from her and stood guard, arms folded.

Ebony peered through the gaps in the wood, just wide enough to reach her fingers through, waiting to see Hunter striding towards her. But the camp had fallen silent.

Where is he? Why isn't he coming to free me? He must be enjoying this too much, she thought, gritting her teeth.

"Tell Hunter I am here!" Ebony said, louder this time. "I need to speak with him." The guard ignored her. "Hunter!" she yelled. "HUNTER!"

"Shut up or I will make you shut up!" the guard barked.

Ebony swore and gave a sigh of frustration, sitting down in her cage on the damp, woodland floor. She would just have to wait for Hunter to find her there. She was no stranger to cramped, cold places.

"Ebony," someone snapped.

She woke with a start and, at first, didn't know where she was. She was lying on a bed of pine needles, a pinecone dangerously close to piercing her eye, surrounded by wooden walls. She sat upright and tried to stretch her arms, but there was no space.

"Ebony," the voice said again.

She turned around to see a man with a long ginger ponytail looking sour. Ebony looked him square in the face.

"We need to talk."

11

"What are you doing here?" Hunter whispered menacingly. "Let her out," he added to the guard, who obeyed him instantly. He offered Ebony a hand and effortlessly pulled her onto her feet.

"Thanks for leaving me in a cage overnight," Ebony said, following Hunter, who began marching across the clearing. She almost had to run to keep up with him.

He glanced over his shoulder to check if anyone was nearby and turned to Ebony, pulling her inside his tent.

He grabbed her shoulder. "Why are you here?" he spat in an undertone.

Ebony almost laughed. What was he so angry about? She was the one who had spent the night locked in a cage.

"I think I want to join the Bounty Hunters."

Hunter dropped his hand from her shoulder. Ebony hadn't even realised how oddly he had been standing until his back went from hunched and tight to straightened and relaxed. His entire expression changed, and a cocky grin crossed his face as he smoothed back his long ginger hair, tied in a neat ponytail.

"Is this change of heart because I stole your ring?"

Ebony stopped short. "No—it's got nothing to do with that."

"Well, you can't have it back. I lost it …"

"No, you didn't. I stole it back."

Hunter laughed. "My plan worked, then!"

"Your plan? What plan?"

"I stole it from you so that you were forced to come and check us out."

Ebony froze and narrowed her eyes. How had she been so stupid?

"So, what changed your mind?"

"It doesn't matter," Ebony replied, trying her best not to show her irritation. "I just—I want to see what it's all about."

Hunter raised an eyebrow like he didn't quite believe her.

Before he could say something arrogant, she quickly said, "but I'm still going to live alone in my camp."

"Okay," he nodded.

"Okay?" She was surprised it had been so easy.

"Yeah. Okay. I'll find a mission for you and we'll see how you like it."

"Okay … How will I know when I've got a mission?"

"I'll come find you. It shouldn't take more than a few days."

"Will I get paid for it?"

"You'll get a share of the profits."

Ebony looked at him quizzically, looking for signs of deceit, but he seemed to be talking genuinely for once.

"What are you staring at?" he said, smirking.

"I just thought you might say something arrogant and make me want to punch you. You usually do."

Hunter grinned.

"Eb, you've known me only a few days. You don't know anything about what I usually do."

Ebony didn't respond. He hadn't said anything arrogant, but she felt hurt, though she couldn't possibly fathom why.

"Why don't you send one of your loyal followers to come fetch me? Their company would definitely be more appreciated," Ebony spat sarcastically and marched out of the tent.

She had to wait four days. She tried to get on with her everyday life, but the anticipation of being called upon for a bounty mission made her fidgety. She didn't care much for the mission itself. But there was a chance she'd be able to gain the trust of one of the Bounty Hunters and get some information on Hunter. Had any of them noticed his weird behaviour? Or maybe he was right; maybe his behaviour wasn't weird at all and she just thought she knew him better than she actually did.

I can't believe I actually liked *him,* she reprimanded herself. *What an idiot.* No, she didn't like him, she decided. She never had. He was an arrogant, rude, snobby, ass. But he was up to something and she had to find out what it was.

She had changed into her dark outfit, ready to disappear into the shadows. She was dressed in all black, had her dagger safely in her boot, and her black mask in a pocket. She stowed her blue ring safely in her den; she didn't want to risk losing it on whatever mission Hunter was planning for her.

She sat on her log, whittling an arrow by the campfire with her dagger, muttering to herself about how she couldn't trust anyone. The arrow was getting thinner and thinner, but she hardly seemed to notice, and the shavings had made a pile by her feet.

"I'm just like everyone else, am I?"

Ebony jumped up from her seat with a yelp and covered her mouth, her eyes wide with surprise. Hunter stood before her, smiling that twinkling, charming smile. She narrowed her eyes at him.

"I've got a mission for you, Eb."

"Don't call me Eb!" she blurted out.

"Whatever you say, Eb." He laughed his barking laugh and beckoned her to follow him. "It's happening tonight, so we'd better get a move on if you want to be clued in."

The arrow she had been making snapped in her fingers. She sighed before collecting her bow and full quiver. She stamped out the campfire before giving her camp a longing look, her eyes turning grey, and followed Hunter through the trees, always staying a yard or so behind. She didn't want him to think they were *friends* or anything.

"What changed your mind, Eb?"

"It doesn't matter."

"You were pretty set on not having anything to do with us only a few days ago."

"What's it to you? I've changed my mind and you got what you want. Why ask questions?"

"So you're allowed to ask questions and I'm not?"

Ebony gritted her teeth. "Do you want me to turn back? I will if you don't shut up."

Hunter looked over his shoulder at her and kept walking.

"Why are you always in a bad mood?" he said.

"I don't like people."

Hunter laughed. "You'll like my people."

"Doubt it," Ebony said under her breath.

They continued in silence until they reached his camp. Ebony followed Hunter into the tent with the round, wooden table. In the light, she could see more of what was inside. The table had a map of the Dwellings carved into it, including the forest. Little clay balls sat across the map, presumably marking territory. In the woods right by the edge of the city was a collection of these little balls. Was there another gang living in Rundlewood Forest?

The table was surrounded by people. Ebony and Hunter joined five men, one of whom she recognised from somewhere, though she couldn't place him: He was tall with short, black hair and a handsome face. There was also a tall stocky man with shocking white hair, cut close to his head. Ebony was the only girl there.

She turned to Hunter and whispered, "Am I the only girl? I thought there were other girl Hunters …"

He looked at her, bewildered. "Did I ever say there were?"

Ebony didn't reply. She turned back to the table and studied the faces around her.

"Everyone, this is Ebony," Hunter said, gesturing towards Ebony, whose eyes turned an embarrassed shade of turquoise. The men around the table stared at her, all with unreadable expressions. She started to wonder if she had something on her face. "She wants to join the Bounty

Hunters, so I thought I'd give her a simple taster mission like this one. She'll need some training to do other missions, but for this one, she should be fine."

Ebony's insides boiled. He'd wanted *her* to join, not the other way around; and she did *not* need training for *anything*. Why was he putting her on a simple mission? He had said she was *good*, hadn't he?

"Ebony," Hunter raised his eyebrows, warning her not to speak out of turn. He pointed at each person round the table in turn. "This is Alby, Darrel, Halsey, Lennox, and Sam."

Sam.

She *had* seen him before. Her eyes flickered to his hand where a large ring sat. He had been the man whispering to Hunter about a young girl …

"And Daya." Hunter said, as a wiry woman with dry, brown hair joined them. Hunter gave Ebony a meaningful stare, as if to say, 'yes, she is *also* a woman.' She eyed up Daya, who glared at her menacingly. "Daya is our Carer.

She'll look after you if you get injured or sick." Hunter smiled at Daya—a private, meaningful smile.

Ebony's attention kept flickering back to the handsome Sam. There was something about him she liked, but she couldn't work out what it was. He smiled at her and her stomach felt funny, like something was fluttering inside her. She tried to smile back but was completely sure she looked like an idiot, grimacing at him. But she had to be wary of him. He had been the other voice of that conversation she had overheard.

"So, the mission," Hunter began. "It's the tail-end of an ongoing saga—we hope. All you've got to do is get the damn sword back in its case without anyone noticing, okay? You've also got to find a small dagger in a wooden box in the dining room."

"I am so sick of this stupid sword," Lennox said.

"Aren't we all," Sam replied.

His voice was deep, but not *too* deep. It was rich and strong. Ebony's stomach fluttered again.

"So, there are six of you. You'll split up into groups—"

"You're not coming?" Ebony blurted out, looking at Hunter with bright blue eyes like he had abandoned her.

He chuckled. "Of course not. You'll actually have to make *other* friends."

Ebony's eyes turned back to turquoise. She promised herself she'd kick him later for that remark.

"Two of you will stand watch outside," Hunter continued. "Another two will keep watch inside, while the other two put the sword back."

"Seems like an awful lot of people for a very simple task." Ebony said, with a smirk.

Sam laughed. "She's got balls, for sure."

"I've got just as many balls as Daya does, I assure you," Ebony replied, watching Sam's eyes twinkle with amusement. Daya did not seem impressed that she had been included in this interruption. Hunter gave Ebony a warning look, but she just smiled at him.

"Ebony, you'll be on watch outside with Alby—"

"I can do more than just be on watch!" Ebony retorted.

"You don't know our ways, so shut up and pay attention," Daya snapped. "You shouldn't be on a mission in the first place."

"What's that supposed to mean?" Ebony retorted.

They glared at each other with contempt, Ebony's eyes slowly turning orange.

"If you don't mind, Hunter," Sam said, slowly, "I'd like to get to know our feisty one, here. And I think I could stop her doing something impetuous. Put me on watch with her."

Ebony's chest fluttered so much she folded her arms and squeezed to distract herself from the bizarre feeling.

"No, Sam. You're our best man here. I need you to lead the group."

"Yes, sir," Sam replied.

Ebony looked up at him, surprised that he would fold so easily.

"Darrel, Halsey, you'll be on watch inside the house. Lennox, you'll be with Sam. That leaves Alby with Ebony."

Alby gave Ebony a smile; one that she was sure was meant to be friendly but seemed a bit pathetic. Ebony gritted her teeth. Why should Lennox get to go with Sam and not her?

"You'll leave at dusk. When you return, we'll talk about the next bit of the mission." He turned to face Ebony and said, "Come find me later. You'll need some better clothes."

As they left the tent, Ebony caught up with Hunter who was striding off across the clearing.

"You haven't told me *why* we're doing this," she said.

He turned on his heel and stood to face her.

"That's because you don't need to know."

"You asked me to join the Bounty Hunters—you practically begged. But now you're giving me the rubbish tasks and not telling me everything about my mission. How do you expect me to work in a team like this?"

"I expect you to follow orders and not ask questions."

"Okay, let me put it like this. I'm on trial as a Bounty Hunter just as much as the Bounty Hunters are on trial for me. If I don't like this mission tonight, I'm gone."

"Fine by me. But just so you know, I've had to pull many strings to get you on this mission."

"Why?"

Hunter stopped walking and turned to face her. "Women aren't Bounty Hunters. I'm breaking a code for you and people aren't happy about it."

"What about Daya? She's just a Carer, but she was invited to a secret Bounty Hunter meeting."

"Daya is not *just a Carer*. Daya keeps this place going. She's well respected here."

"So, you're just like all the Dwellers, here. You think men and women aren't equal."

"*I* don't think that—but, yeah, that is how society works. But with you here, I'm going to prove to my men that women can do more than they think they can."

Ebony didn't know what to say. Was he supporting her or using her?

"Well—I'll be back in my camp, all alone, just how I like it," she spluttered.

Hunter's expression hardened. "You shouldn't live alone. It's not safe anymore."

"Why? Because I'm a girl? I can look after myself."

Hunter's worried expression returned. His shoulders bunched up in stress and his face turned serious. His eyes flickered about the place.

"You don't get it. It's dangerous for *you*," he whispered.

With that, he stalked off, leaving a befuddled Ebony standing in the middle of the clearing.

"It's Ebony, right?" a voice said behind her.

Ebony jumped and found Sam smiling at her.

"Yeah, Ebony Wick—Sam, right?"

"Samuel Sanker is my full name. You want me to show you around camp?"

Ebony shrugged, pretending not to be delighted by the idea, and followed Sam, who pointed out every tent, telling her their uses. Most tents were barracks—large marquees lined with hammocks for beds. Some people, like Hunter, had their own tent, which Ebony thought was profoundly unfair. She couldn't imagine herself sleeping in a large tent full of other people. It seemed too dangerous. She'd never be able to sleep. Hunter's tent, in which they'd had their mission meeting, was one of the larger single tents.

"So how do you know Hunter?" Sam asked as they approached Lake Ava.

Ebony was pretty sure he knew the answer already, but she replied anyway.

"He was my prisoner for a few days when he broke into my camp. He had been watching me work and wanted me to join the Bounty Hunters."

"What is your work?"

"I'm a highwaywoman and I sell my loot in town."

Sam raised his eyebrows. They stood by the edge of the lake, their reflections dancing on the water.

"So, you live in the woods?"

"Yep."

"Who do you live with?"

"No one."

Sam looked genuinely shocked.

"You live alone in Rundlewood Forest? Are you *mad*?"

Ebony laughed. "No—I'm not mad. It's fine living alone. I prefer it."

"But … there are wild and dangerous people in these woods," Sam said in an exaggerated tone, like he was telling her a ghost story.

"Who's to say I'm not one of them?"

Sam smiled at her and slowly shook his head.

"I like you, Ebony."

Ebony laughed again.

"What? I do. I like you. You're different," Sam said, his eyes sparkling.

"Not many people like me."

"Who's to say I'm 'many people'?"

Ebony smiled. She'd never met anyone quite like him and, for some reason, she felt like she could trust him. She hadn't felt that since … well, since she was a child. A shadow passed over her eyes, remembering the last person she had trusted. She had been ten years old.

"Your eyes—I couldn't help but notice—" Sam said, tentatively.

"That they change colour? It scares most people."

Sam smiled. "Are you sure it's your eyes that scare people?" When she didn't reply, he said, "Let's get us some food, shall we?" and gestured for Ebony to follow him.

He headed toward the scoff tent, as they called it, a large tent lined with wooden tables and benches, and walked to a long counter that was laden with food—a spread the likes of which Ebony had never seen. She gaped, then snapped her mouth shut, worried she looked like a goldfish. Since when had she ever worried what she looked like?

Sam grinned at her, clearly happy to show off what the Bounty Hunters could offer. He picked up a chipped, china plate and helped himself to all kinds of food—potatoes in a tomato sauce, chicken soaked in gravy, vegetables Ebony hadn't eaten since she had lived in The Clink. Ebony followed suit and ladled as much food onto her plate as she possibly could. She didn't know if she'd ever get this opportunity again.

"Where did you get it all?" Ebony whispered to Sam as they chose seats on a long wooden bench; one of many. Most were occupied by small groups, a hubbub of chatter filling the room.

"The food? We bought most of it."

"But how? There's just so much …"

Sam laughed.

"We pool together earnings so we can afford all this, and we hire cooks. Some of us hunt."

"You live in the wild, but you don't cook for yourselves?"

"I wouldn't say we live in the wild. It's like a small village here. But, no, I never learned to cook. Never needed to," he shrugged.

"And the cooks are okay to be … you know … associated with your lot?"

Sam gave a hearty laugh. "They *are* 'our lot'! Cooks aren't often treated well in the city. They prefer working for people like us than the rich elite."

They fell silent as they ate. Ebony's stomach soon began to feel full, but she ignored it. She couldn't waste this food. They piled their empty plates on a table in the corner of the room that appeared never to be fully cleared.

"I have to get going on something, Ebony," Sam said. "But I'll see you tomorrow morning. Go find Hunter—he'll probably deck you out with some warmer clothes," Sam said, glancing at her thin, dark rags. She felt her cheeks flush and her eyes turned a pale shade of turquoise.

She watched Sam walk towards a tent across the yard, feeling like a spare part. She didn't want to stand alone with nothing to do, but she also didn't like the idea of asking Hunter for charity.

She took a deep breath and headed toward his tent. She knew he wouldn't let her go on the mission dressed as she was.

Ebony was given a bed in the barracks overnight. The plan was to rise in the early hours of the morning and convene by Hunter's tent. But Ebony had her own task to complete before then. She climbed into her hammock, glancing round at the many men sleeping around her. She seemed to be the only woman in there. Perhaps the cooks slept somewhere else? As discreetly as she could, she pulled her dagger from her boot and put it under her pillow. Snuggling into the blanket they had provided her, she did her best to relax. But she felt nervous every time she heard someone move. All she could hear was shuffling and grunts; a deep snore and a quiet whisper. It was no surprise she couldn't sleep. She had slept completely alone for four years.

She lay in the rustling darkness for what felt like hours. Should she do it now? Or should she wait a bit longer? A grunt from the hammock next to her made her jump. She couldn't risk one person seeing her.

At last, she couldn't wait any longer. If she waited too long, she would lose her opportunity. As quietly as possible, she slipped out of her hammock and put her dagger back in her boot. Tiptoeing out of the barracks, she made her way across the clearing and past the large bonfire, which was still sizzling with heat. Hunter's tent was quite recognisable against the others; it was white and square, while most of the others were round and brown, apart from the two large marquees.

She had reached Hunter's tent unseen. She slid into the shadows and contemplated her next move. Would anyone question seeing her walk into Hunter's tent in the middle of the night?

She had to risk it. She had to find out any information he had on Alastor Bates. Maybe Hunter would have their next meeting place written down? Or maybe he'd have some of Bates' secrets? Even if he had nothing, Ebony needed to know for sure. Hunter had met with Bates; they had worked together. He *had to* have *something* on him. And if he did— anything at all—Ebony had to have it too.

As quick as she could, she dashed into Hunter's tent and gazed around, willing her eyes to get used to the pitch-black darkness. Slowly, she began to see shapes; Hunter's bed, with Hunter in it (*thank the Mother*, she sighed), the large oak table, and a cupboard—but there was something else next to the cupboard ... a dark shape with red eyes.

It moved. Ebony stifled a yelp and almost tripped backwards. Sam was staring at her out of the darkness. Had she imagined the red eyes? She must have. He strode towards her and grabbed her arm, pulling her out of the tent and into the shadows.

"Why were you in there?" he whispered, sounding a bit irritated.

"Why were *you* in there?" Ebony retorted.

Sam didn't answer.

"You won't tell anyone?"

Ebony frowned. "No—I won't tell anyone," she replied.

"Good. Keep this between ourselves. See you in a few hours," he said sharply and disappeared into the trees.

Ebony was left feeling dumbfounded. Why *had he* been in there? Just as she was about to re-enter Hunter's tent, she heard him yawn and get out of bed. The next day had begun.

12

The day was new, but still very dark, as the five Bounty Hunters and Ebony made their way towards town. Ebony hadn't been in town at night for a long time—not since she was a young girl. Hunter had given her a thick, warm cloak and some old walking boots. Despite their age, they were miles better than her own tatty shoes.

They entered the city at the top of the Common Dwellings and made their way through quiet streets, passed familiar sights, like the inn she frequented, The Cloak and Dagger. They walked for such a long time, Ebony wondered where they could possibly be headed.

They were nearing the end of the housing district in the Commons, and soon they were walking alongside the famous Rundlewood River, which ran through the centre of the Dwellings, heading towards the bridge that Ebony had to cross every time she sold her wares in town, though she normally crossed from the other direction.

When Sam turned towards the wooden bridge, Ebony's insides squirmed. She didn't belong on the other side of the river. It wasn't her place to go snooping around the West Dwellings, the business district of the Dwellings. She was a Commoner. The first time she had even entered the West Dwellings was only a week or so ago; and even then, she had stuck as close to the river as possible.

Sam turned to check he had everyone in tow and paused when he saw Ebony's face in the falling light. He ushered them all across the bridge, but Ebony's feet didn't want to move.

"What's wrong?" Sam asked, putting a hand on her shoulder.

Ebony's insides squirmed a bit more.

"I've never really been into the West Dwellings. I'm not allowed to go there."

Sam laughed, but not in a condescending way—in a way that gave Ebony a bit more courage.

"That's total rubbish. You're allowed anywhere in the Dwellings—they just don't want you to know that."

Ebony looked at Sam, who smiled down at her.

"If you don't follow us, I'll push you the whole way," he chuckled.

Ebony forced herself to move and eventually crept onward. Walking into the built-up riches of the West felt like she was leaving her home behind. She glanced over her shoulder, longing to be back in the Commons; a place she understood.

She diligently followed Sam and the others through foreign streets. There wasn't one house to be seen. All around her were tall, brick buildings. The streets were impeccably clean and tidy and stretched wider than any she had seen before. Some buildings had well-kept gardens outside and some streets even had oil lamps hanging on the walls. They walked all the way across the West

Dwellings to the housing district. The houses were big, but not as gross as Ebony had thought they'd be, having heard rumours about them all her life. She had imagined large mansions with hordes of servants and stables for horses. Perhaps that was only in the South Dwellings? These houses all looked alike; a row of buildings with big front doors and luscious front gardens, though some had carts stationed outside.

At last, Sam stopped walking just as Ebony's feet were beginning to grow weary. Sam perched in the shadows on a low brick wall that surrounded the front garden of one of the houses. Ebony went to sit beside him. They all gathered together, waiting for Sam's instructions.

"So," Sam began. "This is the house. There's a back entrance. We'll all need to climb over the gate to the garden. Ebony and Alby will stand watch outside while we get on inside. We're looking for a study with an empty sword case on display. By the end of tonight, the sword case should no longer be empty. We're also looking for a meeting room. On one of the shelves should be a decorative wooden box. Inside is the dagger we want. When we're done, we leave the house as it was and make our way back. Understand?"

The house was on the corner of a street. Alongside it ran a tall, brick wall, in the middle of which was a wooden door held fast by a padlock. Attached to the top of the wooden door was a row of metal spikes. They couldn't possibly climb over the gate. Alby, Darrel, Halsey, and Lennox looked to Sam with defeated looks, as if to say 'what do we do now?' Sam looked up and down the street, trying to think of another way of getting into the house.

Meanwhile, Ebony was digging about in her trouser pockets. "Aha!" she said and was quickly shushed by her team. Before anyone even noticed what she was doing, the gate swung open before them.

Darrel's jaw actually dropped. "How did you do that?" he whispered.

Ebony held up a thin, bent bit of metal. The group looked at her in confusion—all except Sam, whose expression held a wide grin.

"I haven't seen a lock pick in years. Where did you get it?"

Ebony shrugged. "Nicked it from an orphanage when I was six."

Lennox looked impressed, but disgruntled. He clearly didn't like being upstaged by a girl. Ebony was surprised to find the back door to the house open. Darrel, Halsey, Lennox, and Sam disappeared into the house and left Alby and Ebony standing outside in silence. Ebony glanced around the garden and took a peek into the house through the windows, but it was so dark she couldn't see much. Alby stood guard like a soldier on duty. The minutes passed by very slowly. An owl hooted. Ebony sat on the grass, but soon, inactivity made her cold. She went to stand next to Alby, who just stared straight ahead, and looked at him until he finally returned her gaze.

"So. Alby, huh?"

Alby raised an eyebrow in expectation.

"Your name's Alby? Short for … Albert?"

"Nope. Just Alby."

"Huh."

Alby turned his head away again. Another few silent minutes passed.

"You been with the Bounty Hunters long?"

"A few months."

"A member of the Dwellings guard before then?"

"How did you know?" he replied, turning his whole body to face her. She had finally got him to relax.

"Just a hunch …"

After another minute of silence, Ebony found herself getting bored.

"How long have they been? It seems like they've been gone ages."

"They'll be back soon."

Ebony huffed. She didn't like being left behind, she decided.

"So why does everyone bow down to Hunter like he's someone to worship?"

"He's our leader," Alby responded.

"Yeah, but doesn't anyone ever question him?"

"He's the best we have. He *made* the Bounty Hunters. Why would we question him? We're in good hands with him."

Ebony grimaced. Did this man have any of his own opinions?

"Right … so he's never done anything to annoy you?"

Alby took a minute to reply. "It doesn't matter. He's our leader. What he says goes."

Ebony gave up. It was useless trying to pry a personality out of him.

After another five minutes of awkward silence, she couldn't handle it anymore.

"I'm going in," she said.

"What? You can't! We have to stay outside!"

"Who cares? They're taking too long. Something's up. Keep this safe," she said and placed her bow and quiver by his feet. She couldn't risk knocking anything by accident and making too much noise.

Before he could stop her, Ebony opened the back door and entered the dark house. It was bigger on the inside than it seemed, all made up of long, thin corridors lined with paintings and doors. At the entrance of the first corridor, Ebony could see something lying on the ground—no, *two* somethings. She approached with caution to find two dead guards; their throats slit. Straining her ears, she tried to listen for any sound, but couldn't hear the others. She quietly checked each room as she passed by, trying to find any sign of the rest of her team.

At the end of a long corridor was a large, square room, decorated with floral blue wallpaper. In the middle of the room was a long table, a huge painting framing the wall behind. There was one set of shelves in the corner of the room. Just as she was about to continue on through the house, Ebony took a step back, remembering the second part of the mission. Maybe this was the meeting room?

She made her way to the shelves at the back of the room and searched for a wooden box. There were a few, but none were very decorative, except a long thin one on the very bottom shelf. The box was carved like it was made out of ivy. Pulling it out, she opened it. Inside was plush, yellow silk, holding a long, thin dagger. It wasn't as beautiful as her own dagger, but it was a dagger in a meeting room, in a wooden box, on a shelf. And she had been the one to find it.

She took the knife, put it in her belt, and put the box back in its place. Standing up, she turned to leave the room and return to Alby, but as she did so, her shoulder knocked the shelf. It rocked dangerously and, before she could do anything to stop it, something made of glass fell and smashed into a hundred pieces at her feet. It felt like the sound echoed throughout the entire house. Ebony winced and quickly made her way out of the meeting room and back the way she had come. She was walking down one of the long, thin corridors, when a door opened before her.

A man in a long, light blue dressing gown appeared, holding an oil lamp.

Ebony couldn't believe her eyes. There he was; standing right before her, in his dressing gown. Alastor Bates. She was *in* his house. Her heart lurched. She had been waiting for this opportunity for years. But she didn't have the right weapons on her; she was completely unprepared. The pair stood still, suddenly very aware of each other. Ebony wondered if he recognised her. But how could he? She had been so young. An image flashed through her mind of a small boy being whipped at Bates' command. She couldn't even remember what the boy had done to deserve such a punishment; if he had done anything at all.

"Help!" Bates shouted at the top of his voice. Another door opened at the end of the corridor. A young boy not much younger than Ebony appeared in a raggedy nightshirt, brandishing a letter opener, desperately trying to look menacing.

Ebony turned on her heel and ran back down the corridor, back to the meeting room. She took the first exit she could and sprinted through the house. She could see a big door before her and could hear members of the household opening doors upstairs. Almost tripping over another dead guard, she wrenched at the large door before her and found herself at the front of the house. Quietly closing the door behind her, she hid behind a hedge in the front garden, catching her breath. She had given up her best opportunity—maybe even her only opportunity. And for what? To help the Bounty Hunters? *Or maybe I'm just a coward.* Should she go back in and try again? By now, Bates would have sent a message to his guards and she would soon be surrounded. She may have squandered this opportunity, but at least she now had something she didn't have before. She knew where he lived. Promising to pay him a visit in his sleep, she made her way to the back garden where she could hear voices.

"Where the hell is she?" Lennox growled.

"Alby, you said you'd stop her doing anything stupid," Sam said.

"What happened in there?" Halsey asked. "How come they all woke up?"

Before Alby could explain what had actually happened, Ebony appeared by the gate, with an apologetic smile on her face.

The team seemed less than impressed. The house was awake now. They could hear voices from inside.

"We need to go!" Sam whispered.

Alby shoved Ebony's bow and quiver into her hands without looking at her and followed Sam's lead. Nobody but Sam seemed to know where they were going. They sprinted after him, turning left and right past rows upon rows of houses. Ebony kept an eye on Lennox's white hair, which was so white it almost seemed to glow in the dark. Up ahead was a line of trees. Ebony took a huge sigh of relief when her feet crunched on dry leaves. They continued into the forest until Sam stopped running, leaning on his knees to catch his breath.

Ebony scanned the trees around her. She didn't know this place. And, it seemed, neither did the others.

"What the hell happened back there?" Halsey demanded.

"Everyone in the house woke up and saw us," Darrel said. "But how did they hear us? We were dead silent."

"Sam and I got the sword back in its place, but we didn't have enough time to find the dagger."

"Alby, what happened with you two?" Sam snapped.

Alby tried to mumble a response, shooting furtive glances at Ebony.

"You're weak, Alby. You can't even control a young girl," Lennox spat, with a smirk.

Alby didn't seem to know how to respond.

"It wasn't his fault," Ebony spoke up. "I got bored of waiting so I decided to come find out what was taking you so long."

The team fell quiet and glared at her like she was mad.

"I told Hunter he shouldn't have put me outside."

Lennox turned to face her.

"You broke protocol because you were bored? Hunter said you were *good*. He clearly doesn't know you very well."

"You were taking ages with quite a simple task—" Ebony retorted.

"If you can't work as a team, you shouldn't be with the Bounty Hunters."

"That's exactly what I've been saying to Hunter all along." The group fell silent. Before anyone could respond with another angry remark, she added, "But I got the dagger."

"You what?" Sam said.

"I got the dagger. I found the meeting room, got the dagger, and headed out," Ebony said, brandishing the dagger she had found.

"You're sure that's the one?" Sam asked, taking it from her.

"Well, it looked like a meeting room, there was one set of shelves, there was a long, thin wooden box—the only decorative one—and inside was this dagger." Ebony shrugged. She decided to leave out the fact that she was the reason why the entire household had awoken.

"So, we did it?" Alby said.

"We got the sword back, we got the dagger, but we didn't do it without being seen," Sam said. "But, hang on a minute, Ebony. How come you came out the front door and didn't just go back to Alby?"

"I—I was looking for you lot—I didn't want you to waste time looking for a dagger I'd already found."

"So, you don't know why they all woke up?" Halsey asked her.

Ebony frowned and shook her head. "I guess you weren't as quiet as you thought you were."

"Or maybe *you* were the one who wasn't quiet," Lennox said, giving Ebony an obstinate glare.

"Look, she got the dagger, didn't she? And we didn't. Who cares who woke them up?" Sam said. "Let's just find our way back."

The walk back to the camp was a long one, but when they reached it, everyone still seemed to be sleeping. Sam showed Ebony to his tent and made a rough bed for her in one corner out of blankets and clothes. She was too tired to wonder why Sam was privileged enough to get his own tent.

Ebony was awoken by the sound of swords, laughter, and voices. For a minute, she had no idea where she was. Had people invaded her camp? Why was there so much noise? She sat up and rubbed her eyes as Sam walked in from outside.

"Morning, sleepyhead," he winked at her and went to collect some supplies for his daily duties. "Hunter wants to talk to you." He stopped to give her a charming smile, then strode off across the clearing.

Ebony's stomach churned and growled with hunger. She ran her fingers through her hair and stretched her arms and legs. It felt weird to be able to stand next to her bed.

She blinked and squinted in the morning sunlight as she made her way over to Hunter's tent. He was staring in concentration at some papers on his round table and looked up when he heard her arrive. He sighed and shook his head.

"What were you thinking? You went against protocol, you broke the rules, you entered the house when I had specifically told you to stay outside with Alby." He sighed. "What is your problem? They weren't difficult instructions to follow."

"Morning to you, too," Ebony replied, standing firmly in the entrance to his tent.

"I mean it, Ebony. Why did you even think that was a good idea?"

"Who cares? We completed the mission and I got the dagger."

"Sam told me what happened. You didn't get it unseen, did you? You don't realise what a mess you've made by simply being *seen*." Hunter held his clenched fists close to his sides.

"Well, I *might* understand if you told me what the mission was about." Ebony paused. "And who's to say that was my fault?" she asked, her brow furrowing.

"That group has been a team for a long time and they're some of my best people. Only when you join them and break protocol does the mission go wrong. I'm not stupid, Ebony."

Ebony glared at him with a scowl.

"I told you I don't work well in a team."

Ebony glared at Hunter. She had warned him this would happen, but he hadn't chosen to listen to her. He wouldn't even give her credit for getting the damn dagger.

"You didn't even try," Hunter snapped. Ebony turned to leave. "You're not done yet," Hunter said. She stopped in her tracks and turned to face him, her eyes a deep shade of orange. "You still need to do the exchange of goods tomorrow."

"See you tomorrow, then," she snapped.

Before he could reply, she turned on her heel and marched away from him, across the clearing and into the trees, until she could no longer be seen.

13

Ebony spent the night in her den but rose with the birds. The bivouac was crisp with cold and she could see her breath in the air. She needed more money. She desperately wished she could stay in her camp, but she knew that if she continued with this damned mission, she might get paid, even if just a small amount. She glanced back at her camp and sighed, then made her way back towards the Bounty Hunters, her bow and arrow on her back. By the time she got there, only the cooks were awake.

Ignoring their intrigued expressions, she ladled a pile of ready-made breakfast onto a plate; eggs and toast, sausages and bacon. They were certainly prepared to feed the masses here.

Daya, the Carer, scowled at Ebony as she walked past, before helping herself to some breakfast and sitting on the furthest table away. It wasn't long before Ebony was joined by two others; Darrel and Halsey. Darrel sat beside her and Halsey sat opposite. Ebony put her bow and arrow on the floor under her legs.

"Hunter's not used to people like you," Halsey said, grinning at Ebony, before helping himself to a large sausage off his plate.

"I think it's good for him," Darrel said. "He needs someone to question him once in a while."

"Alby didn't think so last night," Ebony mumbled.

The pair laughed. "Alby's a dunce," Darrel said, then shovelled toast into his mouth.

Ebony grinned. Had Hunter purposefully kept her apart from these two? They seemed a bit more willing to bend the rules. Perhaps Hunter thought she needed to learn from the most loyal Hunters first.

Ebony placed three fingers on her forehead and closed her eyes, saying the Fae words of grace in her head. If she was ever going to fit into this place, she wouldn't be able to perform Fae rituals like she normally did. At least, not out loud.

"Is Hunter always so bossy?" Ebony asked, changing the subject.

Halsey shrugged. "He's the leader. He has to lead. But when you get to know him a bit, he can be a laugh. Though I don't think anyone *really* knows him."

"I get the feeling he's a man with a lot of secrets," Darrel added. "So, what's your story, Ebony?" he asked, genuinely interested.

"Umm—I grew up in The Clink—"

"Yeah, so did I," Halsey interjected.

"Then I left—escaped … I think I was about ten. Lived on the streets in a gang for a while, but two years ago I moved into the forest. Made myself a camp, learned to catch food."

"You learned to cook for yourself out here?" Halsey asked, his eyebrows raised.

"I was taught to cook in The Clink by a matron. I think she felt sorry for me." Ebony wasn't ready yet to tell anyone the full truth. Matron Hilda had been like a mother to her until the fire had taken her.

"Sounds like you've got some interesting stories up your sleeve," Darrel said.

Ebony smiled but didn't reply. She didn't know if she could trust them yet, however friendly they seemed.

"So … Daya," Ebony said, changing the subject. "Bit snappish?"

"Aw no," Halsey said. "Daya's great, she just has a thing for Hunter. I reckon she's jealous of you—and she likes being the most important woman here. Doesn't like having a contender."

Ebony chuckled. "You think I'm a contender?"

"Well—you're the first female Bounty Hunter. Hunter is changing the rules for you, so you must be as good as he says."

Ebony smiled. She wasn't used to being complimented.

"Darrel, weren't you supposed to be on a mission this morning?" a passer-by asked, stopping at their table and eying up Ebony with a mixture of curiosity and suspicion.

"Yeah—but it got cancelled. Donahue didn't go away in the end. They say he got ambushed by the Demon," he said nonchalantly, but Halsey looked nervous.

Donahue. Hadn't Ebony heard that name somewhere before?

"What about his wife?" Halsey asked, genuinely concerned.

"Yep—her too. She swears she saw a moving shadow with blazing red eyes. It attacked their cart and left them for dead."

Ebony almost laughed. Even the Bounty Hunters believed in the Demon. She felt in her pocket for the blue ring she had stolen from Lord Donahue's carriage and turned away to hide her face, afraid they'd ask her questions, suspecting that she might know more than she was letting on. But what did the Bounty Hunters have to do with the Donahues? Were they stealing *for* them or *from* them?

They soon finished up breakfast and headed towards Hunter's tent. Daya was there, talking with Hunter in an undertone, looking very serious. Ebony thought Hunter looked a bit irritated.

"So, we're all here now, yes?" Hunter said as Lennox joined them.

Ebony glanced around, wondering where Sam was.

"Sam got called away on other matters," Hunter said, as if he could read Ebony's mind. Ebony nodded without looking at him, feeling a bit awkward about their row the night before. "Alby won't be on this mission," he added. "This one is very easy, but I'm sending four of you—firstly, to teach Ebony how an exchange is done and secondly, because I don't trust this guy we're delivering to—he may have armed men watching you. All you need to do is collect the money and replace it with the dagger. All clear?" They all nodded. "Off you go, then."

Ebony checked that she had enough arrows in her quiver before the four of them began the trek away from the camp, Lennox leading the way into a part of the woods Ebony didn't know. They walked for about an hour, Halsey grumbling about the cold.

"Could've given us horses, at least," he mumbled.

"Get a grip, Halsey," Lennox snapped. "You're a Hunter, for Pete's sake. Act like one."

Ebony couldn't tell if Halsey had turned red or if his cheeks were just cold.

At last, Lennox stopped. Through the trees, Ebony could see a small stone plinth, on top of which sat a large brown bag of coins. Lennox pulled the dagger they had stolen from his belt and walked towards it. Ebony went to follow him, but the others stopped her.

"Only one person does the exchange."

"Why?" Ebony asked, but the others shushed her.

"There could be men watching us," Darrel whispered to her, his eyes furtively searching the trees.

Lennox reached the plinth, hauled the sack of money under his arm, and replaced it with the dagger. He tentatively stepped away.

Ebony heard a rustling in the trees behind her and, in half a second, had an arrow drawn. Halsey had a dagger in his hands and Darrel had his hand on the hilt of his sword, ready to draw it at a moment's notice.

A figure in black appeared from behind a tree and ran towards Ebony. Without a second thought, she let loose her arrow and hit him square on the forehead. He fell to the ground with a thump.

"Nice shot," Halsey said.

Darrel went to inspect the body.

"This isn't one of his men," Darrel noted.

At that moment, they heard Lennox cry out and the sound of steel against steel. He was surrounded by three more men, all dressed in black.

Darrel charged towards him, his sword drawn. Ebony found a bush to crouch behind and tried to aim, but Darrel and Lennox moved so fast, she was worried she would hit the wrong person.

With a deep breath, she aimed. Her arrow whistled through the trees and hit one of the men in the back. He collapsed on Lennox, who was busy fighting another. He stumbled and almost lost the fight, but Halsey, who had disappeared into the trees, leapt into the fray and slit the throat of his adversary just as Darrel finished off his own. The woods fell silent.

"Ebony?" Darrel called into the trees. She rose from behind her bush and went to collect her arrows.

"These aren't his men, are they?" Lennox said.

"Nope. Someone knew we were here."

"So, what do we do now?" Halsey asked. "Can we trust that he'll get the dagger?"

They all paused in thought.

"I'll stay," Darrel said. "I'll wait here until he comes."

Lennox patted his shoulder. "Just don't let him see you,".

"I won't," Darrel nodded. "See you later," he called as Halsey, Lennox, and Ebony disappeared into the trees. Ebony felt a bit guilty about leaving Darrel behind in the cold but shivered and welcomed the idea of sitting by a warm fire.

"So how do we split the loot?" Ebony asked as they walked back to camp.

"Umm—" Halsey looked awkward. "Hunter said to split it between him, me, Lennox, and Darrel ..."

Ebony stopped in her tracks. "You mean I don't get any?"

Lennox and Halsey stood shuffling their feet, not daring to look into her eyes, which had turned a dark red.

"Is it because I broke the rules? Great Mother, that man is difficult!" Ebony slowly shook her head in disbelief. "Tell him, if he wants anything from me, he knows where to find me," she snapped and disappeared into the trees, making her way back to her camp.

14

Ebony sat relighting her small campfire as the light fell around her. Muttering to herself, her face flushed, a vein throbbed in her forehead. The fire sparked flames and her camp was almost whole again. Almost, but not quite. Ebony looked around, wondering what she had missed. The den was there, the fire was lit, her weapons were close by, her traps were set … so why did it feel so different?

Turning back to the fire, she began boiling the broth she had started to make the morning before, accidentally dropping her ladle in the flames and wincing when she had to fetch it out again.

"I'm perfectly fine here on my own. I don't need anyone else to do missions with," she told the trees. "I have survived alone since I was ten. I don't need fancy blankets or—"

"Or what? What else don't you need?"

Ebony actually yelped this time. She spun on her heel, dagger in hand, to find Hunter smirking at her.

"Go away, Hunter."

"I came to apologise."

"I don't need your apology."

"You don't need much, it seems."

"No. I *don't* need much," Ebony snapped. She turned back to her fire, doing her best to ignore him.

"You were right. You told me you don't work well in a team and I ignored you. I had to learn the hard way. I'm sorry, you clearly don't want to be a Bounty Hunter, so— I'll just leave you alone now."

Ebony huffed and threw some small twigs on the fire, most of which missed or hissed, letting off a strong burning smell. After an uncomfortable silence, she heard him turn away back into the forest.

"I thought the Bounty Hunters were supposed to be ruthle2ss? That's what they all say. The whole team were a bunch of cowards last night."

"They also say you're a demon from the Shadowlands," Hunter said, before turning back into the trees.

"I *can* work in a team, you know," she blurted out. "I just choose not to." She looked over her shoulder, but Hunter had already gone. Ebony sighed. Why did he annoy her so much? So what if he wouldn't pursue her anymore? She had other things to care about.

She ate her hot broth out of habit, but she didn't really want it. She wasn't very hungry, and it had started to rain. She crawled inside her den and huffed. Everything had been so simple before Hunter had arrived.

That night her nightmare returned.

She was in a dormitory full of sleeping children, and she was the only one awake. The bed on her left was empty. She glanced at it in confusion.

Where was he?

The paint was peeling on the walls and the door had a fist-sized hole in it. She peered through the hole into a long, drab corridor with faded carpets. She turned to go back to her bed, but the room had turned a deep orange. Flames licked at the walls and spread across the floor like water. Children were screaming. She couldn't see them, but she could hear them. They were all screaming as the flames encircled her from floor to ceiling.

And then, in front of her appeared a young boy—he must have been about seven. He was standing enveloped in flames, his hands blackened and his clothes disintegrating. His face was slowly melting away until only his mouth was left. He smiled at Ebony like nothing was happening.

"Henry!" Ebony screamed. "Henry, you're on fire!"

"I stole some cookies from the kitchen. Want one, Eb?" He held out his blackened arm, the flames holding the shape of his body like a new layer of skin.

"Henry!" Ebony screamed so loud her voice broke. Tears flooded her face as she leapt forwards ...

She sat bolt upright with a gasp, sweat dripping, tears running, head throbbing. Taking a deep breath, she reached out for the hilt of Henry's dagger that she always kept beside her and curled up tight, staring into the darkness of night.

Her breakfast was salad made from whatever edible leaves she could find. It was time to start stockpiling for the winter. She spent the day foraging for fruit and vegetables in the nearby trees, storing them in pots in her shelter. It felt good getting back to the normal swing of things. She emptied her traps and set new ones, aware that when the food shortage set in, outlaws in the woods could get dangerous. She had to protect herself as best as she could. She had only caught one rabbit, which would do for dinner. She needed to make more traps and collect more meat to dry above the fire. She still had a small amount of pork left from the boar she had killed, but it would need to be dried and preserved with salt before it went bad. She'd have to buy some salt the next time she was in town.

After skinning her rabbit and preparing it for dinner, she washed in the stream while the rain fell and later dried by the fire, smelling the deliciously damp forest. All the while, she performed as many Fae rituals as she could remember; determined not to forget the way she had lived for the last two years. With red berry juice, she drew symbols on her arms and chest, protecting her from dark woodland spirits, and prayed to The Mother using the Fae words of peace.

"Peace be to the Mother and her daughters. Peace be to the forest and its trees."

She went to bed in a more peaceful mood than the night before, listening to the rain start up again.

The next day was the coldest of the year so far. The frost was thick and the clouds were an odd shade of pink. The carts rumbling through the forest would be scarcer now that the ground was slippery with ice. It was time to settle in for the winter. She rose early and spent the day scavenging. The next morning, she headed into town to buy what she could—though, at this rate, she knew she'd have to choose between extra food or a warm blanket.

She crossed the bridge near the Common Market and froze. She looked around with wary eyes. She was sure she had seen movement out of the corner of her eyes. The bridge stretched over the river that ran through the Dwellings. On either side were run-down buildings, blackened with age. She made her way down the dark street that led to the market but stopped again when she heard feet shuffling down an alleyway. She drew her dagger from her boot and slowly turned around, looked up at the rooftops, and peered down nearby walkways.

As she turned to continue walking, she felt a hand grab her shoulder and a blade at her back. She let the hand drag her into a dark alleyway, before she was shoved against a wall. The dagger's owner was a big and burly teenager, with very short bristles of hair. One eye was blue, while the other was brown. He leered at her.

"So, you *are* still alive?" he grunted.

Ebony looked at him sourly. "Haven't you heard? I'm a Demon from the Shadowlands."

The boy looked at her sternly, then he grimaced—or was it a smile?

"I thought that might be you," he laughed.

Ebony smiled. "Gren, why are you still holding a dagger? Daggers aren't your weapon of choice."

Gren shrugged. "Orders. They want words with you," Gren said, gesturing her to walk ahead of him up. The streets were so narrow in this part of town, it would be a squeeze to walk side by side. There was no use trying to escape. Ebony knew there would be other urchins keeping watch as they made their way to the Leader of Ebony's old gang; Black Jade.

"What have I done?"

"You've been seen with Hunter Sparrow. The Jades think you've been keeping things from them."

"And do you think that?"

"I think you're mixing with the wrong people."

Ebony laughed. "They're better than the street gangs!"

Gren grabbed her shoulder. She was sure he meant to grab it reassuringly, but he had never really known his own strength. He turned her round to face him and looked her squarely in the eyes.

"They might seem nice now, but they're not safe. Secrets are more dangerous than you think."

"I know what I'm doing, Gren."

He smiled and sighed. "You always did." He reached out with his right hand and knocked on a small glass window. A door nearby opened a notch and Ebony followed Gren inside. The building they entered was dark and grimy, with years of filth layering every surface. A group sat huddled by a mouldy couch at the back of the room; all of them aged sixteen or under. A beast of a boy stood, towering over everyone else.

"Ebony Wick," he grunted. Ebony hadn't met the new leader yet, though she had heard about him on the grapevine. He was known for his brawn and bloodlust, but not so much for his brain.

"That's me," Ebony said, raising her eyebrows expectantly. Most people would likely fear being surrounded by a street gang like this, but Ebony knew most of its members and their fighting tactics, and she knew she was faster than any of them.

"We need to ask you a few questions as a fellow member of The Jades."

"I'm not a Jade. Sorry to disappoint."

"Once a Jade, always a Jade," one of the boys piped up; a small, skinny boy called Archie.

Ebony laughed. "You wanted me chucked out once."

"These are new times, Wick," the Leader said. "And you're a Bounty Hunter now."

Ebony shook her head. "Got that wrong, I'm afraid. They didn't want me, either."

"We have seen you with Hunter Sparrow."

"You know Hunter?" Since when did the Bounty Hunters let themselves be known to lowly street gangs?

"Tell us their secrets," the Leader grunted.

"I don't know any of their secrets because I am not one of them. I worked with them once, just so I could steal some information from them—that's it."

"What information?"

Ebony frowned. "Hunter works with Alastor Bates."

"You're not still on about *that*, are you?" Gren rolled his eyes.

"I don't get it—he whipped you," she pointed at Archie, "starved you for a week," she pointed at a tall, gangly boy, "cut your hair off because he said you looked better as a boy," she said, pointing at a round-faced girl with startling blue eyes. "Why *don't* you want revenge?"

"It's not that we don't want revenge," Gren said. "He's too difficult to get at."

Ebony nodded. "And that's why I'm working with the Bounty Hunters. They might be able to help."

"If you're gonna keep working with them," the Leader grunted, "You're gonna be a spy for us."

"Why? What's in it for me?"

"We can make your life in town very difficult if we want."

Ebony sighed. She had been mostly ignored by the street gangs up till now. But if she wanted to trade ever again, she'd have to work with the street gangs—if only minimally. *Damn Hunter.* This was his fault.

"Fine. I'll let you know if they tell me anything of importance—anything I think could be of use to you."

The Leader glared at her. "We'll be watching." He nodded to Gren, who led Ebony back out into the alleyway and towards the market.

"Where did you get *that* one from?" Ebony chuckled once they were out of earshot.

"Bryn is actually quite a good Leader. He may be a bit thick, but he's good to us."

Ebony raised her eyebrows in disbelief but changed the topic. "I didn't see Charlie. Where is he?"

Gren stopped walking and looked at Ebony, sorrow in his eyes. "The Snatchers—well, they'd been looking for him for a long time. Number one on their list for *years* …"

"What happened?"

"They got him—sent him to The Clink, but—well, you remember Charlie. He wasn't good with authority."

"What did they do, Gren?"

"Bates got to him."

Ebony paused. "What do you mean?"

"He was thrashed in the square till nightfall. By the time we found him …"

Ebony felt something heavy lodge in her throat.

"He's dead, Wick."

Ebony blinked away the tears threatening to sting her eyes and took a deep breath.

"He can't keep doing this, Gren." She shook her head.

They continued walking till they reached the end of the alleyway.

"Stay safe, Wick," Gren said, before leaving her alone once more. But Ebony hardly heard him. She couldn't get the image of Charlie tied up and bloody ... Her heart felt sore. Her eyes flashed a brilliant red and she turned back towards the bridge, anger in her stride.

She knew where to go now. She knew how to find him. Alastor Bates wasn't long for this world.

15

Ignoring the knot in her stomach as she crossed the bridge and continued into the West Dwellings, Ebony gritted her teeth. She didn't belong in the West, but she didn't care anymore. She didn't belong anywhere.

The houses soon became bigger and more lavish, but everything looked different in the daytime. She could see the detail in the front gardens; the decorated porches and the grandeur within. The upper class sickened her. How could they live like this knowing that half the city lived in abject poverty? She had heard the South was even worse.

Her determination grew with every house she passed. Bates was at the centre of the depression in The Commons. She passed through the sparkling clean streets, lined with oil lamps ready to be lit for nightfall. She kept the image of Bates' house in her mind. Even though it had been dark, she was quite sure she could still find it. And soon enough, there it was, with its brick walls and the wooden back door. It didn't take long for Ebony to pick the lock and get into the back garden. It was bigger than she remembered: a luscious, green lawn with a picnic table and chairs, filled with green bushes, flowers, and a few trees. She scowled. She would need to wait for nightfall before breaking into the house. She found a bush at the back of the garden that was just big enough to conceal her and settled in for a cold, uncomfortable stay.

She woke with a start. The world around her was dark and the stars shone brilliantly above. It was a cloudless night; cold and harsh. There was a stillness in the air and the city had gone dark. The house loomed before her, almost menacingly. She stood up and walked towards the back doors. It hadn't been that long ago that she had stood right there with that dunce, Alby.

She softly turned the handle of the back door. It was locked. With a deep breath, she began picking the lock and, eventually, heard it click. The door swung inward. She took a step over the threshold and into the dark house and, as quietly as she could, made her way through the long corridors, retracing her steps. The house didn't make a sound. It seemed everyone was asleep.

She came upon the meeting room with the shelves at the back of it. It had two doors leading off it—but which one had she taken before? She crept over to the shelf where she had found the dagger and her grey eyes peered through the darkness at the two closed doors before her. She hadn't even noticed the second door last time. She couldn't be in this house too long—she didn't know if he had set any traps since her last visit. One of the doors led to a long, thin corridor and Bates' personal chambers. She pictured herself smiling down at a sleeping, vulnerable Bates, holding a dagger to his throat.

She opened one of the doors and a long corridor lined with more doors stretched before her. Sighing with relief, she tentatively stepped into the hallway. She was looking for the fifth door on the right—or was it the third? Maybe it was the fourth? Her heart began to pound in her chest. Which door had he appeared from?

Damn rich people and their giant houses. She gritted her teeth and took a deep breath. She'd have to guess. She tried the third door on the right. The door opened quietly and revealed what looked like a games room with a doll's house and a rocking horse. She closed the door and tried the next. It creaked as she opened it. A woman was sleeping in a bed; she looked old and peaceful. Ebony closed the door. *Third time lucky.*

The next door opened into another bedroom, decorated with dark wood. There was a large four-poster bed, but no one was in it. She heard a stir from one of the rooms and shut the door with a clunk. She stood still in the hallway, hoping she hadn't woken anyone.

The house stood still. *Where was he?* She had been sure he had come from the fifth door. She tried the next door, but it only led to a small broom cupboard. The next was where the boy had appeared from. The corridor ended there, leading to a small staircase. Her palms felt sweaty and she began to feel very thirsty. *Maybe he hasn't gone to bed yet? Maybe he's in a different room?*

She retraced her steps and found her way back to the meeting room, closing the door behind her, then approached the second door. She tentatively reached out for its handle, which turned with ease. She pulled the door toward her and found a large study, lined with hundreds of books. It had a huge, round stained-glass window depicting the sun, and directly beneath it was a large, oak desk, piled high with papers and opened books. Behind it sat a man, slumbering in a tall, wooden chair. Ebony's heart skipped a beat and her red eyes shone in the darkness. He was there before her; vulnerable and unarmed. She tiptoed through the room, before reaching for the dagger hidden in her boot. She paused. It was too perfect; too easy. She glanced around the study. Was anyone hidden, ready to attack? But there was no one to be seen.

Her hand felt slippery as she gripped her blade and made her way around the desk, towards the man she hated the most. She normally didn't like to kill, but this one was different; this one deserved it. She crept closer; her dagger poised. One more step and she would be close enough.

Thunk. Something under her foot had moved.

She heard a grinding noise somewhere behind her and spun around to see the bookshelves turning, opening like doors, revealing dark figures that began to swarm into the room. Bates sat up with a jolt and Ebony leapt towards him. She just needed to reach his throat.

Something pulled her arms backwards as Bates yelled and leapt up from his chair. She leapt forward with a cry and swiped the air with her blade, catching Bates' cheek. He cried out in pain and cradled his bleeding face as Ebony was dragged away from him. She twisted around—it was the boy she had seen before. Without hesitation, she drove the dagger into his chest, and he fell with a cry, letting her loose.

"Peter!" Bates shouted in anguish.

Ebony lunged towards Bates again, but several figures barred her way, swords drawn. She retreated, trying to see where the door to the study was through the darkness.

"Who is it?" Bates barked into the darkness.

"The Shadow," one of his guards replied.

"That is *not* the Shadow," a voice said from across the room. Sam's voice. Ebony froze.

The men turned towards him, giving Ebony the chance to disappear into the shadows.

"Who are you?" one of the men barked.

Sam drew his sword. *What is he doing?* Ebony thought to herself. *He will never be able to fight them all!*

She lunged out of the darkness towards Bates, but he was quicker this time, his arm striking her face with such force, she staggered back. Bates' face was contorted with fury.

"You're no Shadow. You're just a girl," he seethed.

She heard a cry from the other side of the dark room and the ring of steel. He was right before her, but just out of reach. She had only seconds to make her choice.

She lunged with her dagger, which grotesquely sank into Bates' skin. She pulled her dagger free and watched him fall to the floor. Blood gushed from his side as he clutched at the wound with both hands. Ebony looked up. She was surrounded by his guards and wasn't armed to handle them. The room froze and everyone stood watching Bates bleed out onto the floor, gasping for breath. Only a few steps away was one of the secret doors, still open and revealing a set of stairs, descending into darkness. There was no other way out. She retreated and disappeared into the darkness. She paused halfway down the stairs—*Will Sam be okay?* —she continued running. She had to get out of there. *How did he get here in the first place?* She couldn't stop picturing Bates on the floor, blood pooling around him. *How had Sam known where I was?*

The stairs eventually came to an end, leading to a door. She wrenched it open and stumbled onto the street, gasping for air. She found herself at the end of a row of houses—the end of Bates' road. How had she got there? His house wasn't *that* big. She leaned against the tall brick wall beside the door she had just emerged from. She had done it. She had found Bates and killed him—well, she had mortally wounded him, at least. So why didn't she feel anything? She didn't feel triumphant joy or even anger. She felt empty. She began to walk up the steep road, back towards Bates' house. She would retrace her steps from there and slowly find her way back home.

But someone grabbed onto her hand and shoved her hard, into a wall.

"What the *hell* were you thinking?" Sam whispered into her ear through gritted teeth. "You could have been killed. In fact, I'm amazed you're still alive," he spat. "You could have been tortured for information!" He pulled away from her and waited for an answer.

"How did you know where I was?"

Sam faltered. "I—I saw you in town looking suspicious. I followed you."

"I hid in Bates' garden for hours ... why didn't you show yourself?"

"It doesn't matter how I knew where you were. What matters is that we get out of here. Now." He grabbed hold of her wrist and started dragging her back down the street. "I finished him off for you, by the way," he said as she shook herself free of his grasp.

"I didn't kill him?"

"No, you didn't. He might have died from blood loss eventually, if he hadn't been treated in time." Sam was walking fast with quick strides. Running would make them look suspicious.

Ebony felt deflated. She had done it all wrong. She hadn't got the satisfying revenge she had dreamed of. She hadn't even killed him herself.

"Why were you after him anyway?" Sam asked as he directed her through the streets of the West Dwellings.

"He's Alastor Bates," Ebony said, as if the name said it all. "He had it coming. He's the leader of the Snatchers."

"The Snatchers?" Sam asked, as if he'd never heard the word.

"You know, the Common Custodians – 'keepers of the peace' and all that. With Bates gone, the Snatchers won't have their leader."

Sam scoffed. "So they'll pick another one."

Ebony's head span. "But he practically *created* the Snatchers. He's the ringleader."

"They're not a gang, Ebony. They're a police force. They'll get a new leader in a week or so."

Sam looked at her as he walked, but Ebony just looked ahead, her expression steely.

"You want to take down the Common Custodians?"

"And him—I wanted to take him down."

Sam raised his eyebrows. "A personal vendetta. Interesting."

"And yes. I want to take down the Common Custodians."

"You won't be able to do it alone," Sam said. Ebony stopped walking as Sam turned to her. "What? We have to keep moving, Ebony."

"You don't think I'm crazy wanting to take them down?"

"I think you're crazy trying to do it alone."

Ebony continued walking, quickening her pace. "Most people think I'm crazy for even considering it."

"I told you before, I'm not like most people," Sam replied.

Ebony laughed. He was right about that. They eventually reached the trees. Once they were out of sight of the Dwellings, Sam stopped walking.

"I can help you, Ebony. You're going to need to work in a team, though."

Ebony's turquoise eyes shone through the darkness.

"I'll see you around," she said and left him staring after her as she made her way back to her camp.

16

The day before felt like a dream. Had they really killed Bates? Would it make any difference? It hadn't had changed anything in Ebony's life. She was no safer in town.

In fact, she felt a bit stupid. Had she really thought that killing him would change things? She sat staring into her fire, occasionally poking it with a long stick. The silence of the frosty trees was deafening.

Biting her upper lip, she watched the flames dance and wondered what she should do next. So much of her energy had gone into her revenge for that man. What did she have now but a tiny den in a vast forest?

A list began forming in her head. *I've got food, water, a place to call my own. I get to do things* my *way.* She stood up abruptly. "Stop moping!" she snapped at herself out loud.

Leaving her bow and arrows hidden safely under the roots of a tree, she headed into the trees, unable to walk quietly anymore, since every leaf was frozen and crackling underfoot. She collected sweet violet leaves for salads, stinging nettles for tea, cutting the stems with her dagger, and the remaining sloes and rosehips. Her goal was to survive, she decided, and, for that, she needed food for the winter.

Sitting beside a hedge growing juniper berries, she saw movement in the trees. It could have been a deer, but she would never be able to hunt it without her bow. She tucked her dagger in her boot and began walking back to camp, but something felt odd. Was somebody watching her? She stopped walking, wary that if she was being followed, she was leading them straight to her camp. She glanced around the trees, but all was still.

Then out of the trees, three large men appeared and, with a war cry, leapt at her. Ebony tried to reach the dagger in her boot, but she wasn't quick enough. A large man with short blonde hair tripped her up and held her down, her face scraping against the frosty earth. She writhed and screamed, while another man tied her wrists behind her back. The third man stood watch.

"Stop moving," one of the men grunted. She felt a heavy kick at her ribs and gasped for breath.

"Let me go!" she yelled, her heart racing. "What do you want?"

Were they really this desperate for food already?

There was no answer. They hauled her onto her feet and checked her for any hidden weapons. They searched her jacket pockets and her bag of gathered fruit and vegetables, which they threw to the ground and left forgotten. Satisfied with their search, they roughly pulled Ebony through the trees, away from her camp.

"What do you want?" Ebony snapped at them, the cold wind stinging the fresh cut on her face.

"Be quiet," one of the men grunted.

"Why? Why should I be quiet?" Ebony said, talking as loudly as she could, hoping that anyone nearby might hear her. But the forest was too vast.

"Just tell me what you want, and I might be able to give it to you," Ebony said, fearing the worst.

One of the men halted her and reached into his pocket. He retrieved what looked like a handkerchief and tied it around Ebony's face, gagging her. This wouldn't keep her quiet, though. She wriggled in the vice-like grip of the blonde man and made sure to be as noisy as possible. She received a harsh punch to the stomach and doubled over, coughing into the gag.

"That's what you get for being so goddamn noisy," he barked at her.

Ebony quietened down from then on, taking stock of her surroundings, trying to work out where they were headed. They were walking North in the direction of the Bounty Hunters' camp. These men weren't Bounty

Hunters though, or were they? Was she part of a mission? What could they possibly want with her?

Feeling her dagger in her boot, a hiding spot they had forgotten to check, she made herself stumble. Over the next hour or so, she became as clumsy as she possibly could, desperately hoping that they would stop and give her a chance to reach into her boot. But they ignored her, dragging her roughly through the shimmering trees, lined with a layer of frost. The walk was a long one, and the light had already begun to fall when she spied the Bounty Hunters' camp up ahead.

They walked straight into the training ground in the middle of the camp, standing beside the large campfire. They stopped and gripped Ebony's arms. A tentative crowd began to form before her, watching and waiting for something to happen.

"Hunter Sparrow!" the blonde man yelled. "Hunter Sparrow! Come and collect your booty!"

A murmur ran through the crowd.

"Ebony?" a voice said. She turned to see Darrel watching. Ebony tried to make a cry for help, her wrists aching and numb with cold, but one of the men gave her a kick to the shin, causing her to fall to the cold, hard ground.

"Hunter Sparrow!" the blonde man called again, louder this time.

At last, Hunter showed his face. He forced his way through the crowd that was growing by the minute and surveyed Ebony on the ground, wrists tied, mouth gagged.

"What do you want?" Hunter said, his eyes darting about the clearing.

The three men turned to face him and drew their weapons. Now was her chance. Ebony leaned back and stretched her fingers behind her as far as they could reach. She could feel it—the pommel of her dagger was just visible. Straining her fingers, she pulled the dagger out of her boot, doing her best to not let the three men see what she was doing.

"We demand ransom for this girl. If you don't pay up *now*, we will kill her."

What kind of people are these Hunters? Ebony wondered, gazing around at the onlookers. She would have charged in by now. But Hunter hadn't given them the go-ahead, so they all just stood and watched. With her dagger, Ebony began to saw at the ropes binding her wrists.

"We want fifty gold coins for her release."

"Fifty?" Darrel said loudly. "And where are we supposed to get that from?"

"Darrel, I'll deal with this," Hunter called to him from across the yard.

The rope on Ebony's wrists snapped and she let it fall to the ground.

"I'll pay it," Hunter said, in a commanding voice that everyone could hear.

Ebony froze. *Is he serious?* she thought, a look of confusion sweeping over her face. Was he really willing to give them that much just for her? Why? The crowd appeared to be asking themselves the same question.

"Come with me," Hunter said. "I promise no one will harm you, and I will give you the money. Just let her go."

"Give us the money first," the blonde man barked.

It was now or never. Ebony swung her arm forward and stabbed at one of the legs standing before her. It buckled and a shocked cry filled the air as one of the men fell to the ground. A cheer went up in the crowd. Twisting around, the man thwacked Ebony's head with a fist. She felt herself fly backwards and the world went dark. When she came to, her jaw was throbbing and she could feel blood streaming from her nose.

Sam had appeared from nowhere, his sword drawn. The blonde fell, his eyes staring at Ebony as their light went out. She blearily got to her feet and dodged a thickset arm swinging at her face. With a quick sidestep, Ebony slashed at the third man's chest and withdrew her small blade as he staggered back and fell with a thud. She collapsed on the ground in exhaustion, every bone aching with cuts and bruises.

For a second, the camp was utterly quiet. But the stillness didn't last long. The crowd erupted, cheering with a roar. Hunter gazed at the chaos in the middle of his camp with a dazed expression.

"We need to clear up the bodies," Sam said, untying Ebony's gag. "You okay?" he asked.

She nodded, her stomach fluttering. He had saved her when the others had done nothing.

"Go and talk to Hunter," Sam said. "He can get you a hot drink. Darrel and I will deal with this mess." He called over to Darrel as Ebony stumbled towards Hunter.

Hunter grinned at her. "You always have a trick up your sleeve, don't you?"

17

She woke, lying on what appeared to be a large pile of pillows, brown from overuse. Slowly, her vision came into focus. She was in a green canvas tent, big enough to stand in, which was held up in the middle by a tall, wooden pole. There were other beds in the tent, but they were all empty. By the entrance sat Samuel Sanker, asleep in an uncomfortable-looking chair.

Ebony croaked and Sam jerked awake, giving her a warm, wide smile.

"Thank God," he said.

"Where am I?" Ebony mumbled. She remembered walking with Hunter to his tent, but not much after that.

"You sort of blacked out in Hunter's tent. You went all dizzy, so he took you to the medical hut. You've slept a long time."

It was only then that Ebony realised it was light outside—not daytime, but it might have been approaching dawn.

"I've been waiting for you to wake up," Sam said.

"How long have you been sitting there?" Ebony asked. She tried to sit up on her elbows, which collapsed beneath her.

"Most of the night. Hunter had to leave around midnight, so I took over."

Hunter had been watching over her? Perhaps he felt he needed to repay her for looking after him while he was sick.

"You helped me fight off that other man," Ebony said, recalling the events of the evening before. "Everyone else just stood watching. Why did you help me?"

"When that guy punched you, I thought you were out cold. I couldn't let them hurt you like that and get away with it."

"Hunter—he said he'd pay the ransom." She paused, trying to remember what had happened. "But why?" It didn't make any sense. Why did Hunter suddenly care so much for her survival when she had let him down so badly in the mission that he had entrusted to her? Hadn't he finally accepted that she didn't want to join the Bounty Hunters? And why had those men captured *her*? What use was *she* to anyone?

Sam shrugged. "Your guess is as good as mine. Any idea why he cares about you so much?" he asked with an odd expression on his face. Ebony couldn't quite make it out. Was he genuinely curious? Was he also wondering why Hunter cared for a simple, lowly footpad? But there was more to his expression than mere curiosity. He was looking at her as if he wanted her to admit or confess something—but what? What could he possibly think she knew?

Ebony shook her head slowly, her eyebrows furrowed, and she did her best to sit up.

"I want to see him," she said.

Sam pushed her back into her bed.

"No can do, I'm afraid. Not until he comes to see you."

"Why not?" she snarled at him, then instantly regretted it. Had he not sat watch over her all night?

"Because I don't know where he is," Sam replied, matter-of-factly. "And because he said you're to stay in here today and I'm to enforce that."

Ebony huffed in frustration.

The day passed slowly. Hunter appeared in the afternoon with a Carer to take a look at her. The woman, Helen, was wiry like the chief Carer, Daya, but with pale yellow hair. She must have been one of the oldest members of the Bounty Hunters, though Ebony had seen older people in town. The Carer checked her bruises and smothered them in smelly gels made from plants.

Hunter then took Ebony to the food tent and sat while she ate her fill. He didn't talk much. He just seemed happy that she had survived her ordeal. By the time she had finished, the light had completely fallen and the camp was retiring for the night.

Ebony was given an hammock in the barracks again that night, but she didn't sleep a wink, despite the warm blanket they had given her. The bruises on her legs and ribs still ached.

She rose with the sun, which, apparently, was early for a Bounty Hunter. They rose when they felt rested, and some would wake but stay dozing, rising only when their stomachs grumbled with hunger. Ebony sat round the large fire in the middle of the camp. She had wanted to go home after her release from Hunter's tent, but nobody would let her. They said she was safer in Hunter's care.

Soon, the camp began to rumble with noise.

"Ebony," Daya said as she came to sit beside her at the fire. "The whole camp is talking about you; our new recruit."

Ebony smiled shyly, a bit surprised that Daya was talking to her at all. "Not sure I'm a fully committed new recruit just yet."

"I know Hunter can be difficult. But he's a great leader," Daya said. Ebony just shrugged. "I misjudged you, Ebony. I thought you were a petulant child," Daya said, looking at her feet.

Ebony raised her eyebrows, words caught in her throat.

"You have some things to learn—a certain maturity is needed as a Bounty Hunter, especially if you're going to be the only female—I know what that's like … but you have potential."

That was high praise coming from Daya.

"Umm—thanks …" Ebony mumbled.

"So, we know you're worthy of us, but we're all a bit unclear about what happened yesterday. Care to enlighten me?" Daya smiled at her almost too sweetly. For the first time, Ebony got a good look at her face. It was tired and appeared underfed, though it held a natural beauty.

Ebony shrugged again. "I don't know. I was gathering food in the woods when I was ambushed by three men. They tied up my wrists and marched me here, then asked Hunter to pay ransom. God knows why he agreed to it—I expect he had a plan, and I probably messed it up."

Daya chuckled. "He would've wanted to ask them some questions. But you and Sam killed them before he managed it."

"Exactly. He and I think in very different ways."

"But I know Hunter —I know him well," Daya said, as if this was something to show off about. "I thought he was going to charge in and save the day. But Sam did that. It was almost as if Hunter was scared of something."

Ebony shrugged. "Who knows what goes through that man's brain?"

At that moment, Halsey joined them next to the fire.

"Hello, Hero of the Moment," he said, beaming at Ebony.

"Please don't call me that."

"Don't you know who those men were?" he said. Ebony looked at him quizzically, slowly shaking her head. "They were part of The Foryx Clan, our enemy gang."

"You have an enemy gang?" Ebony raised her eyebrows. "But why did they capture *me*? What am I to them?" Ebony asked.

"Who knows—they are a law unto themselves. But let's not get into all that politics now. It's time for breakfast."

Ebony followed Halsey and Daya into the scoff hall but didn't feel very hungry. Everywhere she went, someone she had never met thumped her shoulder or nodded at her. It appeared her stunt yesterday had given her acceptance into this strange village.

As they ate, Halsey, Darrel, and a few others reiterated yesterday's skirmish moment by moment, asking Ebony so many questions she wished she had more answers for them. How had The Foryx Clan even known where to find her? Why Ebony? Why Hunter? Sam was oddly distant, though he gave her a warm smile as he passed her in the food tent. As the day went on, the questions became more probing. "Why was he willing to pay so much for you?" By late afternoon, they were asking, "Why is he suddenly changing the rules about female Hunters?" And by nightfall: "Why do you even matter to him?"

Ebony was sitting whittling arrows with Darrel and Halsey when Daya approached.

"So, how long have you and Hunter been an item?" she snapped at Ebony.

Ebony choked and stifled a laugh.

"An item? No thanks," she said, making Darrel and Halsey chuckle.

"Everyone is saying you're an item and that's why he was willing to pay ransom for you. He didn't even try to negotiate with them."

Ebony looked into Daya's fiery eyes.

"Hunter and I are *not* an item," Ebony snapped.

"I saw you sneak into his tent in the middle of the night."

Ebony paused, wary of Darrel's growing look of suspicion. Someone *had* seen her that night.

"That wasn't me. Why would I want to be in his tent in the middle of the night? Hunter is *way* too old. In fact, I don't really like him—at all. He's a bit of an arse."

Halsey laughed again but sobered as Daya's face grew dark.

"Hunter is a great leader. You don't know *half* of what he has to deal with."

"And you do?" Darrel said, his eyebrows raised.

Daya turned her back and stormed away.

"Never mind her," Darrel said. "She's just jealous. Hunter's never saved her from anyone before."

By the evening, the camp was restless and Ebony had started to receive dark looks that were very different to the faces of triumph she had seen in the morning. In fact, a lot of people wouldn't look at her at all, and conversations quickly hushed as she walked by. Even Darrel and Halsey had begun to give her odd looks. She quickly found herself craving the quiet of her camp. Taking her plate out of the food hall, she found a tent that was stacked high with empty crates and sat on a pile of straw, trying to ignore the murmur of talk from outside. She said the Fae words of grace under her breath just as Hunter appeared.

"I wondered where you'd got to," Hunter said, standing in the doorway of the tent. "Why are you in here and not with the others? I see you've befriended Darrel and Halsey."

Ebony shrugged. "I don't really belong in there," she said, referring to the food hall.

"And there are rumours going around about you and me."

Ebony grimaced. "They liked me this morning, but they don't now. This is why I don't like people—you can't trust them. I told them you weren't willing to pay the ransom—you probably had a plan forming. But they don't seem to believe me."

Hunter sat down beside her and stole a potato from her plate.

"Daya tells me she saw you sneak into my tent at night."

Ebony shrugged. "I was trying to find information on Alastor Bates."

"Bates? Why?"

"To kill him."

Hunter looked at her quizzically but didn't question her. "He was found dead a few days ago …"

Ebony gave a subtle smile. "Yeah, I know."

Hunter raised his eyebrows but changed the topic. "How did you sleep in the barracks last night?" he asked.

"Terribly," she replied honestly, then laughed.

"Why don't you sleep in here tonight?"

Ebony raised her eyebrows, looking around the tent that was clearly a stockroom.

"We could make a little straw bed—I could find you a blanket. Might be easier to sleep if it's closer to what you're used to."

Ebony gazed at him.

"Why do you care so much?"

"Eb, I know I can be annoying—and rude at times. But yesterday you proved to everyone what I have been saying about you—that you're not just a runaway kid. I want you to stay and feel welcome here. But maybe, for now, you shouldn't be out there with them. Just let the rumours die down a bit first."

"So why don't I go back to my camp?"

"It's not safe for you there. The Foryx Clan are missing three men who were tasked with finding *you*. They won't forget this easily."

"Who are The Foryx Clan exactly?" Ebony asked.

"They used to be Bounty Hunters, but they formed their own group with a different leader—Everret Anders, the old leader of the Snatchers. You won't remember him—bit before your time. Bates was his cousin."

"The leader of the Snatchers formed an illegal gang?"

Hunter nodded. "He kind of rebelled against the Dwellings …"

"Why did they leave the Bounty Hunters?"

Hunter sighed. "Long story—one for another time." He stood up. "Wait here, I'll sort out a bed for you."

Not long later, he arrived with a huge pile of straw, which they laid out like a bed, and he filled a small sack with straw for a pillow. He then fetched a thick, fur blanket; just the type Ebony had been dreaming about for months.

18

Ebony woke up to find Sam watching her sleep again. He smiled as she prised open her eyes.

"What are you doing here?" she grumbled, her voice gravelly from sleep.

"I've been given orders to keep you in here."

"What? Why?" Ebony pulled herself upright.

"It's not safe for you out there. The rumours have spread, and people want answers."

"I don't care."

"Well, Hunter does, and I take my orders from him." Sam gave her an admonishing look like she was a schoolgirl who had just broken the rules.

"So, I'm trapped in here?"

"Yes. Until the rumours die down a bit. It's for your own good. Bounty Hunters are trained to discover secrets."

"But I don't have any secrets to keep from them."

Sam looked like he didn't quite believe her. "They don't know that. They're getting a bit ... rowdy. Hunter and I care about you too much, that's all."

Ebony narrowed her eyes. There was more to it than that; there had to be.

Over the next few days, Ebony was kept inside her makeshift bedroom. Sam fetched some more straw for her and kept her company as much as he could, but she still wasn't given any freedom. She didn't see Hunter once. Maybe he was avoiding her on purpose to convince his Hunters that he didn't care about her? Though she doubted avoiding her would do the trick. He was keeping her in a private room, guarded by Samuel Sanker, his most trusted man.

It took five days. Five whole days for Hunter to come and see her. Five whole days since she had been allowed outside. She could feel herself going stir crazy. On the third day, she had tried to escape, but there were guards surrounding her tent. She might have been able to get past one, but not three.

On the sixth day, she lay on her bed, watching the sun light up the morning. She felt strong and healthy, fidgeting with unspent energy. So why was she still imprisoned? Why hadn't Hunter come to see her yet?

Sam had been very attentive—almost suspiciously so; bringing her meals three times a day.

She could hear voices approaching her tent and pretended to be asleep, drawing the fur covers above her shoulders.

"How is she doing?" Hunter said as he approached the tent.

"Bored. She's not used to being cooped up so long," Sam replied as he opened the entrance to her tent.

A minute later, Sam nudged Ebony's shoulder. "Ebony, wake up. Ebony?"

Ebony yawned and stretched, feigning confusion and grogginess. "What is it, Sam?" she groaned.

"Ebony, how are you?" Hunter said. She did her best to act surprised to see him there.

She sat up in bed and turned to glare at him. "How do you think I am, trapped in here?"

Hunter wouldn't meet her eyes and stood rigid, his arms folded. Sam sheepishly retreated to a corner of the tent and stared at his feet.

"Why are you doing this to me?" Ebony snapped.

"Now, hang on a minute," Hunter barked. "You've got a bed, warmth, and food. You tied me up for days and fed me burnt stew and stale bread."

"So that's what this is about?"

"No—I mean ... it's just not safe for you out there right now."

"And since when did you care about my safety?"

At last, Hunter returned her gaze. "Since now. Get used to it." With that, he marched out of the tent, Sam at his heels.

"If this is how you look after people, then I don't want your help!" Ebony called after him. She sighed and slid back under the covers. She needed to work out how to get out of here—soon.

He didn't care about her, he just wanted her to think he did. He was up to something, and she was a part of it.

Well I don't care about him *either. I refuse to be his bounty.* How had she managed to let herself trust him? She had been foolish, thinking they were friends. She felt like such an idiot. *Ebony Wick works alone.*

Ebony spent the day grumbling to herself and even ignored Sam when he came to bring food. When the light had fallen, Sam returned, a bowl of soup in hand.

"Ebony, talk to me." No reply. "I know you're angry—and a bit restless. You just have to trust us right now."

Ebony bristled and rolled over in the bed, turning away from him.

"Eb—"

"Don't call me that," she snapped.

"Why? It made you talk, didn't it?"

"You're starting to sound like *him* now."

"Who? Hunter? He can be a jerk sometimes."

After a few minutes of silence, Ebony sat up and said, "Why am I being kept in here? He doesn't care about me—no one does. What is he up to?"

Sam smiled. "*I* care about you," he said. Ebony felt a flutter in her stomach. "And Hunter does too. He just has an odd way of showing it."

"But why is it dangerous for me out there? I've lived in the wild for years and I've survived." Ebony sat up in bed and accepted the warm soup. The tent was cold, and she felt goose bumps reach down her arms.

"Sometimes people can be more dangerous than the wild. Besides, nobody knew you were out there," Sam frowned.

"What's that supposed to mean?"

Sam paused. "Okay, I'll tell you all I know—but you can't let Hunter know that I told you."

Ebony nodded and sat up straighter, shadows reaching across Sam's face in the dark.

"The people who kidnapped you—The Foryx Clan … well, they seem to think you're important to the Bounty Hunters—I mean, not that you aren't important … but they asked for ransom, and Hunter would have paid it."

"Why doesn't he want me to know that?"

"He won't say … I don't know why. But I do know that the guards outside your door aren't just there to keep you in here—they're also here to keep people out."

"And what are you here for?" Ebony snapped.

Sam gave a wounded frown. "I'm here to look after you."

Ebony thought about that for a moment, but questions began to form in her mind.

"Sam, why did you kill Bates? Isn't Hunter doing business with him? Won't he be angry with you?"

"Hunter's business with Bates is nothing to do with me. This is a dog-eat-dog world we're in. Hunter's client is dead." Sam shrugged. "He'll find another one."

"How—how *did* you kill him? You were surrounded by his guards …"

Sam smiled. "I'm a highly trained fighter," he replied, as if this explained it all.

Ebony narrowed her eyes. She had an odd feeling there was something he wasn't telling her.

"*Why* did you kill him? Why help me?"

"You were in danger, Ebony. I just wanted to help you."

"But why?"

"Because I care about you, of course."

"But *why* do you care about me?"

Sam paused, his brows pinched in confusion. "Umm … because you're my friend."

Ebony knew she had been stupid enough to trust Hunter. What made this one any different? She narrowed her eyes, trying to gauge the truth in his expression.

"And you're *my* friend, I suppose" she lied. "But I don't do the 'friends' thing very well."

"I'll bear that in mind," Sam smirked.

He seemed to have bought it. Any sway with Sam might give Ebony a chance of getting out of here and away from the Bounty Hunters.

"I'll see you in the morning, Eb," Sam said, then corrected himself with a nod, "Ebony." Just before leaving the tent, he paused. "Why don't you like that nickname?"

Ebony deliberated telling him everything but settled with the shorter version of the story. "Someone I lost called me that."

Sam nodded, then disappeared into the night.

It was time for action, Ebony decided. She couldn't sit around anymore waiting for Hunter to release her. She had to take things into her own hands. She had to work out how to get out of there.

The next morning, Ebony took stock of her surroundings. She was in a square tent with a large wooden pole holding it up. The ground was dry with crumbled soil. The room had some empty crates in it and her pillows and blanket. At the end of her bed was an ignored tray of food that Sam had brought her the day before; a bowl of soup, now cold, a chunk of bread, and a flagon of water.

Ebony got out of bed and searched the crates. All she found was a small paper receipt for a bushel of apples and a dry leaf. Pouring some of her water on the ground, she created a small patch of wet mud and dipped the end of the leaf into it. Very carefully, she wrote in mud on the paper receipt.

Captured by Bounty Hunters. Please help.

Hearing the tread of approaching footsteps, she hid the note under a pillow.

"I wouldn't if I were you—unless you *want* to feed the rumours," Sam said outside the tent.

"I don't give a damn about the rumours," Hunter growled and appeared in the doorway of Ebony's tent.

"How are you?" Hunter grunted.

"Cold," Ebony replied. "Would love a hot drink," she said, smiling sweetly.

Hunter ignored her and walked further into the tent.

"I know Sam told you what's going on with The Foryx … and I know you're bored in here. But you're going to have to stay here with us until we can find a better solution or until the situation has been dealt with."

"And what exactly *is* the situation?" Ebony said, covering her arms and doing her best to look cold.

"Sam told you. The Foryx want you."

"But why?"

"They think you're important to me."

"Am I?"

"Not particularly."

"So why do you want to keep me safe? Why did you agree to pay ransom for me?" Hunter didn't reply. "Just so you know, I do *not* appreciate being bought and sold."

"It's lucky I don't care what you prefer, then."

"I thought you wanted me to be a Bounty Hunter? How am I supposed to train if I'm stuck in here? If this is your feeble attempt at getting me to join the Bounty Hunters, it is *not* working."

"I'll get you a hot drink," Hunter grunted and trudged out of the tent.

There was something different about him. When he'd been at Ebony's camp, he wouldn't stop talking. He had been downright annoying. But now he seemed grave and sobered. Something had happened, and Ebony needed to know what it was before she was used as a pawn in one of his hunts.

Sam appeared a while later with a steaming tankard of hot water. "Couldn't find any herbs …" he said.

"Do you have any sugar?" Ebony suggested.

"I can have a look," Sam said, disappearing again. He returned minutes later with a smile on his face. "Found a stash of sugar at the back of the kitchens." He handed Ebony the hot drink. She wrapped her hand around the tankard and took a small sip. Working hard to keep a grimace off her face, she gave an exaggerated sigh of satisfaction.

"What was that you said about rumours?" Ebony asked.

"You heard that then?" Sam sighed. With a frown, he said, "Some of the Hunters are starting to ask questions—the same questions you're asking. Why does Hunter care so much about you? Why is he keeping you in here? Of course, no one is stupid enough to ask him themselves."

"And what are their theories?"

"Some say he's in love with you, some say you're his bounty." Sam shrugged. "I've got to go, but I'll drop in later," he said. Ebony gave him her sweetest smile as he left her in peace.

Seconds later, she was crouched by the edge of her tent. There was a small gap between the tent walls and the ground. Ebony emptied the cold soup onto the ground, washed it out with cold water, and poured her hot sugared water into the bowl, hiding it behind a crate.

If that doesn't bring a fairy, I don't know what will.

She didn't even know if the fairies would help her, but they were her only friends. It only took an hour or so. She could hear the flutter of wings on the edge of the bowl. A little blue fairy hovered, cradling water into her mouth with her hands, a look of glee on her face.

Ebony approached her, careful to not make too much sound.

"Do you know who I am?" she asked the fairy, almost whispering.

Its head snapped up and stared at Ebony with large, round eyes, its wings now still. After a moment, it nodded and put a hand on its heart; a sign amongst fairies for 'friend'.

"I need you to deliver a message to your people." Ebony showed her note to the little fairy. "I need help. Do you think the Fae could get me out of here?"

The fairy nodded.

"But how?"

The blue fairy took one last sip of water and reached out to take the paper from Ebony's fingers. With a nod, her wings began to flutter, and she disappeared with a light buzz. Ebony knew that they only made a buzzing sound when they had something to say. The fairy would do as asked; but would the others respond?

She could do nothing now but wait.

19

After thirty push-ups, Ebony was starting to feel tired. She had grown weak sitting in this room. She ignored her beating heart and did thirty sit-ups. Sam found her at number twenty-three and smirked as he watched her.

"You think you can battle your way out of here with strength?" he said, making Ebony jump. She hadn't seen him come in. He was carrying a tray of bread and stew and a flagon of fresh water. She ignored him until she had counted to thirty. Standing up, she took the water and thirstily drank the lot.

"Someone got out of bed, I see." Sam said, one eyebrow raised. He placed the tray at the end of Ebony's bed as she began thirty star jumps.

"Can't let myself waste away in this cell," she panted.

"This isn't a cell …"

"I'm not allowed out. Therefore, it's a cell."

Sam sighed and looked at her with amusement. "Please stop, you're making me dizzy."

Ebony stood still and glared at him. "Fine, I'll stop. Pass me that stew." She sat on her bed cross-legged and cradled the warm bowl in one hand, eating so fast the stew burnt her tongue. Her stomach rumbled loudly.

"What has got into you?" Sam smiled.

"I could be in here for weeks," Ebony replied with her mouth full. "Not gonna let myself get soft."

She slurped down the rest of the stew and gave a satisfied sigh. Sam was giving her an odd look.

"What?" she snapped, putting the empty bowl back on the tray. "Surprised I'm not ladylike?"

Sam blushed. "Well, yeah, actually. I've never seen a lady act like … like—"

"An outlaw? A rogue? A man? Get over it. I'm no lady. I grew up in the orphanages of the Commons."

Sam raised his eyebrows. "I hear that's a tough place for a child."

"You hear? You haven't been there yourself?"

"I haven't had the misfortune."

"So where did you grow up? By the port?"

"I didn't grow up in the Dwellings. I'm relatively new here."

Ebony couldn't believe her ears. "You're not a Dweller?" She realised her mouth was agape and snapped it shut. She had never met anyone who wasn't a Dweller.

Sam laughed. "No, not a Dweller."

"So, what are you? An Outlaw? A Plainsman?"

"No, none of those."

"Then what are you?"

Sam frowned. "You're not going to like it."

"Why? What do you mean?" In her puzzlement, Ebony had forgotten one option … she froze and let herself gape.

"I'm Human, Ebony."

Ebony stood up and backed away towards a tent wall, arms outstretched before her. The word 'Human' was an insult to the Dwellers, referring to a greedy and selfish, power-hungry low-life.

"But—you're nice," Ebony almost whispered.

Sam didn't seem surprised by her reaction.

"I grew up in Shalo County just beyond the Rundlewood Mountains."

"The closed city?" Ebony whispered. "But the Humans were banished there many years ago."

"I wasn't like them. I didn't belong there."

"But how did you escape?"

Sam smiled, a sparkle in his eye. "I have my ways."

"Why would you tell me this?" Ebony asked.

"Because I trust you."

"But there are people in the Dwellings who would kill you simply for being Human."

"That's why I came to the Bounty Hunters. They accept all sorts here."

Ebony slowly sat back down and tried to look calm, though she was far from it. She felt vulnerable sitting with one of the most notoriously dangerous creatures in Atlaan. But he'd left the Humans—he wasn't like them.

"What are they like? The Humans?"

"As cruel as they say."

"Is everything they say about the Humans true then?"

"I don't know what they say about them here …"

"I was told that the Humans found a way to wield magic and began conquering cities—"

"They began conquering cities before they found magic—though, granted, magic made it easier," Sam interrupted.

Ebony continued. "But when they tried to conquer Memoriam, the Fae defeated them, and the Humans were stripped of their magic and banished to a marsh-ridden land called Shalo—"

"Shalo isn't as destitute as they make it sound," Sam chuckled. "There's a big marsh, yes, but there is also the sea, the treehouse village …"

"—And the Fae created guardians to watch over the Humans."

Sam raised his eyebrows. "Now *that* is a folktale. Not all Humans were sent to Shalo, you know. Most of the Humans didn't want to be associated with the stigma of the Human race, so they declared themselves new races; Plainsmen, Outlaws … Dwellers."

Ebony had heard that said before but hadn't wanted to believe it. Could she be related to a Human?

"Are there any people in Shalo like me?" she asked.

"What do you mean, like you?"

"My eyes …"

"No. I've never seen eyes like yours before."

"Most people are spooked by my eyes—you hardly seem to notice them."

Sam smiled slyly. "I've seen much weirder things than colour-changing eyes, believe me."

Ebony's heart skipped a beat. Not many people dared to say it out loud.

"So how come you live in the woods alone?" Sam asked, changing the subject with a look of innocence on his face.

"I was forced to. Sort of." Sam looked at her with curiosity. "When I was ten, my orphanage ... closed down. I joined the street gangs for a while, but then I angered the wrong person and the gangs turned against me." *Well, that's mostly the truth.* "I decided to live in the forest to get away for a while and kind of just ... stayed there." She had never told anyone her story before. She hadn't really had anyone to tell it to, except Tusting, but he had never asked.

Sam smiled at her before collecting the tray and turning to leave. Pausing by the door he said, "I hope you're not afraid of me. Believe me, I am nothing like the Shalolians."

Ebony nodded and gave him the warmest smile she could muster. This camp was a dangerous place. Who knew what else they were harbouring here? What other secrets did the Bounty Hunters have? She knew she would never find the answers sitting in this tent, and Hunter wasn't about to open up.

If Hunter wouldn't give her any answers, she'd have to force them out of him or get them from someone else. Maybe The Foryx Clan would give them to her? But how could she persuade them to tell her anything? A plan began to form in her mind; a plan that made her stomach twist. Hunter was going about this all wrong. Instead of keeping her safe, or whatever it was he was up to, he was only making her more determined to get in his way. She needed to get his attention, and if being recaptured by The Foryx Clan was the only way she'd get some answers, then so be it.

By nightfall, she was growing restless. The camp had gone quiet for the night, but Ebony was wide awake. She lay under her covers, listening to the forest around her.

Thunk. Ebony sat upright. *Thunk.*

The sound had come from just outside her tent. She strained her ears and heard a small buzzing sound, growing louder. Through the darkness of the tent, she could just make out a tiny figure, its wings rapidly beating.

"Ebony Wick," a small voice said. "Now is the time." Immediately, the buzzing sound ceased and a staff in the fairy's hand began to glow, gesturing for Ebony to follow.

She tiptoed her way out of the tent, ready to attack a guard. But they were lying on the floor, unconscious—or worse. Ebony gasped. How had one tiny fairy managed that? No one was awake and the camp was eerily quiet. She took a deep breath in, relishing the crisp smell of the winter night. She followed the tiny light flitting through the air, but soon paused. "Hang on, just one thing," Ebony whispered.

As nimbly as she could, she made her way to the back of the kitchens and prised the back door open, the fairy flitting about nervously and beginning to buzz. There it was; just where Sam had said. A large bag of sugar.

Heaving it into her arms, she began to make her way toward the trees.

"Time is running out," the fairy said.

"Let's go," Ebony said and smiled with glee. The fairy began to speed through the trees so fast that Ebony had to jog to keep up. But she didn't mind. She could feel the wind on her face once more. She could feel twigs and leaves crunching beneath her feet. She caught glimpses of the stars through the canopies above as she ran.

At long last, she saw her camp up ahead. She was home at last.

20

Waking up in her den, it felt like nothing had ever changed. She beamed as she rose, breathing in the damp woodland air. The night had been so dark, she hadn't been able to see much of her camp. But now the morning sun shone brilliantly over a layer of frost on the ground, sparkling like a thousand crystals. The sky was a clear blue. Ebony didn't care that it was now time to weather the winter months; she was back in her own camp and that was all that mattered. She climbed out of her den and began building a fire, her breath steaming in the wintry air. As the fire crackled, she inspected her camp.

Anyone else in her position would move to a new camp now to avoid being hunted. But, for the first time in her life, Ebony *wanted* to be found. She would move to a new camp when The Foryx had given her some answers. She was also intrigued to meet the former leader of the

Snatchers and find out why he had rebelled against the Dwellings. But, for now, she just wanted to taste normality before The Foryx captured her again. If Hunter came for her, she would be ready for him this time.

As her fire crackled merrily, Ebony bathed in the stream, painting the diamond symbol on her chest to ward off dark water spirits. It would likely be the last wash she'd get this year due to the cold. She also washed her dirty clothes, hanging them over the fire. She dressed in her tunic. It wasn't as warm as her dark outfit, but it was all she had. Grabbing the bag of sugar that she had looted the night before, she poured little heaps of it in a circle around her camp as a way to thank the fairies for rescuing her.

She then reset her traps and spent most of the day gathering any food she could find growing in the woods. She desperately needed to rebuild her stocks for the winter. In the few hours before the light fell, she made some more arrows for her bow.

The next day found her in town. She made her way to the port to a large building where coach drivers lived and worked. She had only been there once before, when she had first met Tusting Hicks. She knew what she was about to do was incredibly risky, but she had no other way of doing it. She needed help if she wanted to be ready for winter.

She waited by the door to the coach house, knowing that Tusting would appear eventually.

"Ebony?" a voice said behind her, after nearly an hour of waiting.

Ebony spun on her heel to see a tall, spindly man walk up to her.

"Hicks," she said, "I've been waiting for you."

"I know. Come with me," he said, casting his eyes around warily.

Ebony followed him through a small square behind a cluster of shops and into an alleyway, at the end of which was a hay barn behind the coach house. It smelled strongly of horses and was surrounded by tall, stone walls. Ebony glanced behind her to check that no one had followed them.

"Where the hell have you been, Ebony?" Tusting said, embracing her. "I was worried. I began to think you might be ..." he looked earnestly at her face.

"You thought I was dead?" Ebony chuckled.

"You've been gone for ages! What's going on? Why are you here?"

Tusting looked at her with genuine worry in his eyes.

"The less you know, the better. I got ... caught up."

"You're okay, though? You're not in trouble?"

"Not exactly, no. It's a long story ... Look, I'm here to get a loot. I wouldn't normally come to you here, but—"

"What kind of wares are you looking for?" he interrupted.

"Food. Or material. I need supplies for the winter."

"I told you before; you can stay at my old Nan's house in the winter—no one lives there anymore—"

"Tusting, I don't want to be in this city. I belong in the woods, you know that. Besides, if the Snatchers find me—"

"You don't know?" Tusting interrupted her.

"Don't know what?"

"Alastor Bates ... he and ten of his men were found brutally murdered in his house. Nobody knows how they died."

Ebony looked at her feet. "Wow. How—how do you know?" she asked, forcing herself to look up at him.

"It's all anyone can talk about."

"Brutally slaughtered, you said? How so?"

Tusting gave her an odd look—confusion mixed with worry. "Umm ... I don't know the details," he said slowly. "But apparently there was a lot of blood ..." He paused. "They've appointed a new leader, apparently. Bates' brother, Donovan. They call him a sadist," Tusting grimaced.

Ebony did her best to hide her expression. Of course, Sam had been right. They hadn't taken long at all to find a new leader. But how had he killed all those men? A trained fighter was one thing … but he had been one against ten. She knew he had been hiding something from her.

"It's not safe for me here anymore, Hicks," Ebony said. "They'll be even worse than they were before. And they probably have a drawing of me on file by now."

"Maybe they don't. To them, you're just another street urchin," Hicks said, hopefully. "Besides, they've called in all the Custodians for training. There won't be any on the streets for the next few days."

"I'm more than a common street urchin, and they know it. I'm one of the wild people they tell stories about. I'm the demon with red eyes, remember?" Ebony gave a grim smile, but Hicks laughed. "I just need a few more loots and then I'll—I'll have to stop coming into town for a while. Could you find a carriage or two for me?"

"Fine, I'll do my best," Hicks said. "But that stubbornness will get the better of you someday." He paused. "Wait here. I'll see what I can find." With a reassuring pat on her shoulder, he disappeared.

Ebony perched herself on a hay bale, rubbing her hands together to keep warm. It didn't take long for Tusting to return, and he was carrying something.

He handed Ebony a thin, worn, brown blanket made from some kind of fur.

"What's this?" she asked.

"Just take it," Tusting replied, forcing it into Ebony's arms.

"Is this your blanket?" Ebony looked from the blanket to Tusting in confusion.

"My *spare* blanket—"

"I can't take this …"

"I sleep inside. I don't need it. But you could *die* out in the cold."

Tusting crossed his arms and gave Ebony a stubborn glare.

"Thank you," she smiled, and Tusting's jaw dropped.

He quickly snapped it shut and stammered, "You're—you're welcome."

"So—any loots coming my way?"

"Oh—yes. A spice cart a week from today around noon—you can't use spice for much, I know, but it can sell well. And the villages in the Peregrine Plains are starting to stock up for the winter too. There will be carts every day for the next week."

"I only need a few carts."

"Two days from now is probably your best bet. It's supposed to be feeding a winter solstice event in one of the villages. It will have meat, vegetables … a good mixture."

"Great, thank you. So how can I pay you?" Ebony said.

"By staying alive."

"Hicks, I always pay you."

"Not this time."

"But why?"

Tusting paused and took a step away from her.

"I'm just glad to see you alive."

Ebony's heart twisted. There was that look in his eye again—the look she always chose to ignore. She would tell him how she felt soon—after she'd found her answers. She couldn't return his feelings, and she had been stringing him along for too many years.

She turned to leave, bundling the blanket under her arm.

"Oh, and Ebony?" Tusting said. She looked over her shoulder at him. "I'll be driving the spice cart next week."

She smiled at him and nodded, then made her way back down the alleyway.

21

Ebony slogged her way through the forest towards the main path, the sack on her back almost full, containing everything she owned and the goods she had looted over the last week since she'd seen Tusting at the port. All that was left was the blanket Hicks had given her, a cooking pot, and a bowl, hidden in a sack under a fallen tree, and her dark outfit, which she wore. She would have to make do with just that for the next few days. When she eventually returned to her camp, she would need a few supplies to get her going, but she couldn't afford to risk having all her belongings taken by The Foryx Clan when they eventually found her.

There had been no sign of The Foryx all week and she was starting to grow impatient. At first, she had loved being back home, running her own fire, catching her own food. Meat was growing scarce as it got colder, but she had managed to catch a rabbit or two. But the nights were cold and too quiet. She hadn't realised how noisy the Bounty Hunters' camp had been at night; the distant chatter in the food hall, the rustle of people going to their tents. She had grown used to it so quickly.

Most of the forest was hibernating now and fell into a slumbering, eerie stillness when darkness fell. She could almost hear the silence. It was unnerving. But more unnerving was the fact that she didn't like it. She had always loved quiet solitude, but she found herself replaying Sam's visits in her mind.

Why haven't The Foryx found me yet? And why hasn't Hunter come to find me? I expect he has finally given up on me.

Cursing under her breath, she admonished herself for enjoying the prospect of seeing someone; anyone. Was she looking forward to seeing Hicks? That had never happened before. Ebony was a solitary being.

"I don't need the company of others to be happy. Stop being so stupid," she grumbled. She stopped walking as she felt her feet touch a rougher surface. She had reached the woodland road without even realising. She retreated back into the trees and hid her sack behind a bush. Placing her black mask over her face, she took a deep breath and listened. She could hear a carriage trundling her way and soon she spied Tusting leading it with two horses.

It wasn't long before she had an arrow pointing through the door of the carriage at a large, fat man adorned with rings and a thick coat lined with fur. By his feet were three large pots.

"Stand and deliver," Ebony said in a bored voice. She had done this more times than she could count.

The fat man looked like he could cry.

"Just give me those three pots of spices and you can be on your way," Ebony said.

"B—but I'm under strict orders to give these to—"

"I don't care who they're for," Ebony snapped, pulling back her bowstring.

"Okay, okay," the man spluttered. He proceeded to climb out of the carriage and place the pots by Ebony's feet. Just as he began climbing back into the carriage, Ebony stopped him.

"I want your coat, too. And your rings."

The man looked down at his chubby hands and back up at Ebony, tears in his eyes.

"Not my wedding ring, please ..."

Ebony sighed. "Fine, you can keep that one. Put the rest in your coat pockets and hand it to me."

He did as asked, then made his way back into the carriage and closed the door.

"Now stay there until your driver says you're safe."

Ebony put the spice pots and the fur coat in her sack—they only just fit. When she knew only Tusting could see her, she gestured for him to follow her into the trees. At her request, he climbed down from the carriage and approached her, out of sight of the man in the coach.

"What is it, Wick? What's going on?" he whispered.

"Hicks, I need a small favour. I might be gone for a while—"

"Gone? Gone where?"

"Trust me, the less you know, the better. I'm sorry to be asking for another favour, but …"

"Spit it out, Wick. Something is up, I know it is. You're in trouble, aren't you?"

Ebony sighed. "Could you take this sack and hide it? I might be gone for a while—I don't know how long—and when I get back, I'm going to need this stuff—it's just food and some loot, really …" Before Hicks could argue, she added, "Just keep this stuff safe for me, please." She looked into Tusting's eyes and saw them etched with worry. "I'll be fine, I promise."

Tusting heaved a sigh. "I'll keep it at my Nan's house. Come find me when you're back."

"Thank you so much. I owe you one." Fighting against her instincts, Ebony gave him a quick hug. As he climbed back onto his coach, Ebony looked down at her hands. It felt odd to walk away empty-handed after a loot.

"Wait," she said, remembering the blue ring on her finger—the same ring she had looted weeks ago. With a heavy heart, she slipped it off and handed it to Tusting. "This too. Keep it safe."

Tusting admired it for a moment then slipped it into his jacket pocket.

"I'll see you soon," he whispered to her. Ebony retreated into the trees. "We're safe now!" Tusting called out. "The bandit has gone!" he said, as he drove off down the path.

Ebony was set to have an uncomfortable few days, but it was time to get things going. If The Foryx couldn't find her, she'd just have to make it easier for them. She didn't cover her tracks when she got back to camp. She even wandered further afield than necessary, leaving her tracks for all to see.

She then began to take down the traps that surrounded her camp. Perhaps they hadn't figured out how to get through them yet?

When the night grew dark, she put her fire out and lay in her den, shivering, despite Tusting's blanket, and listening to every sound. But she could hear nothing. Were they really that stupid? she wondered. She was practically a sitting duck, but they still hadn't found her.

After many hours, deep into the night, Ebony still hadn't fallen asleep. She sat up and grumbled. Mumbling with irritation through her chattering teeth, she climbed out of her den and re-lit her fire. She slowly felt feeling return to her hands, and her blue lips turned a pale shade of pink. She sat staring into the flames for so long, her head began to drop onto her chest.

Half-asleep, she heard a rustling nearby. She was alert in seconds. The rustling grew louder and now she could hear whispers in the trees. They had found her at last.

22

Through her tired, blurry eyes, Ebony could see little lights twinkling in the trees. She glanced around, expecting burly men to come charging into the clearing any minute.

Glowing, hovering orbs seemed to be circling the trees and balancing on the ends of branches, like large luminous snowflakes, lit up somehow in the dark. Ebony rubbed her eyes, but the more she blinked, the more the trees began to sparkle and glow. She gazed in wonder, her mouth dropping in awe. It was beautiful. There were stars in the trees all around, winking at her. Was she dreaming?

A soft buzzing noise approached her; a lone star floating through the darkness.

"Ebony Wick," said a small voice.

Ebony jumped and wearily gazed into the trees, searching for the source of the voice.

"Ebony Wick," it said again, crackling and slow with age.

This time, Ebony knew where it was coming from. The floating light lingered a few feet from the ground. Squinting, she focused her eyes. A small, dark fairy hovered before her, its wings buzzing.

"Welcome to the Gathering, Ebony Wick. We are here to protect you."

"Protect me from what?" Ebony asked, in a tired, dreamy voice.

The clearing lit up brilliantly, the twinkling lights in the trees shining so brightly, it seemed almost daytime. Ebony could now see the fairy before her. She had never seen a *purple* fairy before. She was old and wore a floating crimson gown that billowed in the slight breeze. Upon her head was a crown made from tiny leaves and in her hand was a staff with a glowing stone at the end of it. A loud buzzing began, like a swarm of bees. The sound made Ebony shiver.

"We are here to protect you," said a thousand voices at once.

The clearing fell silent. Only one pair of wings could be heard.

"What are you protecting me from?" Ebony asked the trees. There was no reply. Ebony looked to the fairy before her and repeated her question, but the fairy's wings had fallen silent; she would not reply.

"You may call her 'Your Majesty'," said another voice. A young, male, green fairy appeared next to the old fairy.

"I—I'm sorry. I apologize. Your Majesty," Ebony stumbled. "What are you protecting me from?"

"I am Coralia, Queen of the Fairyfolk," said the old fairy. "We have come to protect you from The Foryx and The Hunters."

Ebony looked at the pair quizzically, then glanced around her as the twinkling lights departed the trees and drew in closer. It looked as if the sky was falling. The ground was soon carpeted in twinkling and glowing lights and the trees became as dark as the night. Every fairy had their eyes on her.

"They do not respect you nor us," the Queen said.

"Who?"

"The Foryx. The Hunters." She spoke slowly, almost as if it was difficult for her to speak.

"Do you mean the Bounty Hunters?"

"The Hunters," Coralia affirmed.

"Well, thank you, Your Majesty, but I don't need protection from the B—The Hunters. They're sort of friends, in a way."

"Exactly," Coralia replied in her slow voice.

"Exactly what?"

"They are not friends."

"Well—it's complicated. I don't think Hunter is a friend, but Sam is."

"No."

Ebony sighed. After a long pause, she asked, "Why are you protecting me?"

The Queen and her green companion gave her a look of bewilderment.

"We always have," she said, as if it was obvious.

"What do you mean?"

"You protect us. We protect you."

Ebony thought back to the fairy she had rescued when she was eight and the little fairy she had looked after the other night. She always made sure to leave food and sugar out for them, and sometimes she had melted frozen water for them to drink. She had quickly learned and adopted their rituals. It helped her feel connected to the forest.

"So why didn't you protect me when those men dragged me to the Bounty Hunter camp and tried to ransom me?"

"We didn't know."

She warily gazed at the pool of light now surrounding her feet. She had always thought fairies were harmless, but they seemed oddly intimidating in full force.

"The Hunters and their rivals are the enemies in the war. You must not—" the green fairy said.

The Queen tapped him with her staff as if reprimanding him for saying too much. He bowed and went silent.

"What war?" Ebony asked.

The clearing became still. It seemed they had said all they were going to say on the matter.

"They are coming, Ebony Wick," said the green fairy.

The clearing buzzed with sound again and a thousand voices echoed, "They are coming."

"We must prepare," said the Queen. Every fairy in the clearing turned away from Ebony to face the trees.

"Who is coming?" Ebony asked, bewildered.

"The enemy," said the green fairy without turning to face her.

"Which enemy?"

The green fairy looked over his shoulder with impatience. "The Foryx Clan," he said, then turned away again.

"But—wait, what are you going to do?"

"They will not take you again," said a deeper voice. Another fairy appeared before Ebony, dark as the night. He was dressed in armour and also wore a crown on his head.

"King Alvero," the green fairy said without turning around.

Ebony stood up, surprising herself. "No—you can't protect me. You don't understand. I *want* to go with them—I *want* them to take me".

"This is not possible," Alvero said as if it were a fact. "You will be unsafe."

"Yes—I know. That's kind of the point. I've been waiting for The Foryx to appear … I have prepared for my absence. That's why I left the sugar for you, so I can feed you while I'm gone."

The King smiled, with true warmth in his eyes. "This is why we protect you. You care for our kind, unlike other Humans."

Ebony almost spluttered. "I am *not* a Human."

"Perhaps not," the King replied. "Perhaps you are a rare Human."

Ebony couldn't believe what she was hearing—no fairy had ever been so bold and rude.

"I'm not *Human* at all," Ebony said loudly. "I am a Dweller," she added.

The King smiled. "No matter. We protect you and you protect us."

No matter? Does he not know what the word 'Human' means? Ebony had to stop herself from arguing back.

"You must sleep now, Ebony Wick, and be prepared," the King said, then fell silent.

It seemed that Ebony didn't have a choice. She sighed, then climbed into her den. A fairy followed her in and, somehow, this time, she fell asleep in minutes.

She was in a bed again in a large, decaying room full of many beds—but these beds were hammocks somehow tied up to the walls. In every hammock was a sleeping child. She was the only one awake. The hammock on her left was empty and she glanced at it in confusion. Where was he?

She approached the door to the room and peered through the hole in the centre of the door, but beyond it was just forest. There was no corridor, just thick, dense trees. She yearned to be out in it, but the door wouldn't open.

She sighed and turned around to go back to her bed, but the room had turned the colour of deep orange. In fact, the room was now a large tent—a marquee, lined with hammocks. Flames licked at the canvas walls and spread across the forest floor, racing towards her. Children were screaming. She couldn't see them, but she could hear them. The orange inferno encircled her from floor to ceiling.

In front of her appeared a young boy—Henry. Next to him stood Hunter and Samuel Sanker, all three of them enveloped in flames. Their hands were blackened, and their clothes were disintegrating. Henry smiled at Ebony like nothing was happening. Hunter smirked and Sam winked.

"Henry!" Ebony screamed. "Henry, you're on fire!"

"I stole some cookies from the kitchen. Want one, Eb?" He held out his blackened arm, the flames holding the shape of his body.

"You should join us, Eb," Hunter said, smirking. "You're good at surviving." He looked around at the wall of fire, which was advancing on them by the second, and watched as the blaze licked up his arms, intrigued.

"I'd love to have you on the team," Sam winked at her. She felt her heart skip a beat and pulled her attention from him to gaze at the young boy, whose face was slowly melting away until he had only his mouth left.

"Come on, Eb! Let's sneak into the kitchen!" He laughed so joyfully, she wasn't sure he was even aware of the fire.

"Henry!" Ebony screamed so loud, but no sound came out. Tears flooded her eyes as she leapt forwards to tackle him to the

ground. She would do anything to put those flames out. But just as her arms reached him, he burst into a pile of ashes and she fell—

"Henry!" Ebony yelled. Her heart was racing so hard she could feel it in her chest, and her tears fell freely. She was shaking and staring into the blackness of night.

A scuffling noise came from behind her, somewhere in the nearby trees. Calming her racing breath, Ebony sat as still as possible, waiting to hear another sound. She heard a whisper.

Curses raced through her mind and she quietly searched the darkness for her bow and arrow and the dagger she always kept near her pillow. But all she could feel was damp earth beneath her.

She could hear footsteps around her camp, now. Big, heavy footsteps. They weren't trying to be quiet—or else they were really bad at it. There were at least three men outside. She could hear steel ring against a metal sheath as someone drew a blade. In desperation, she huddled into the corner of her den. If she couldn't see them, they wouldn't be able to see her, right? They'd hopefully think the den was empty and then she could ... do what? She hadn't planned any further than that. She was helpless against such big men with no weapons. Would they attack her? Would they take her back to the Bounty Hunters?

Someone was crouching down and looking straight at her.

Suddenly, the den was flooded with light and Ebony could see her dagger. She had kicked it to the other end of her den in her sleep. She looked into a large, scarred face, her eyes wide. It was a muscular face that reflected the burly shape of the body. He could hardly fit inside her bivouac.

He then pulled away and the clearing outside her den lit up in a flash. Ebony heard a cry of pain and a heavy thud.

The clearing plunged into darkness. An arm reached into her den and grabbed her leg. She yelped and tried to wriggle free but was dragged out onto the frozen forest floor.

Suddenly, the clearing lit up so brilliantly, Ebony closed her eyes tight and the scarred man shaded his eyes behind an arm. When Ebony opened her eyes again, there was pandemonium. Rain had begun to fall in sheets and tiny bolts of lightning shook the air around her. She saw a figure yelping in pain as three more men appeared behind him. They pushed their way into the clearing, swatting at the fairies who had begun to swarm around them, lightning shooting from their staffs. A fairy flew past Ebony's face, its face contorted with rage—so contorted it almost looked like a different creature. Ebony looked at the fairies around her and almost cried out in shock. Their soft, rounded features had become angular, bearing long, sharp fangs. Their sweet, soft hands had become talons, and their eyes were red and piercing.

Ebony could have got to her feet, but she found herself rooted to the spot, watching in awe—an awe mixed with horror. She had never known violence in the Fairyfolk. What had come over them?

Two of the men collapsed to the floor, twitching, including the man who had dragged her from her den. But the third, the largest of the three, swatted away the fairies like they were flies. He waded through the sea of wings and clasped Ebony's arm. Without fighting, she let him pull her to her feet as he dragged her through the swarm and away from her camp, the fairies following, a stream of light through the trees. The forest was so dark and the rain so dense, Ebony could hardly see a metre ahead. Her heart raced, wondering if she had made a mistake.

She looked back towards the light. But the fairies had stopped moving. They all hovered silently, staring into the trees ahead of them. They began to hum as one, and the sound grew louder and louder. With a droning growl, the fairies all sped away through the trees in the opposite direction, leaving Ebony and her captor in the pitch-black forest, the rain soaking them to the skin.

23

The forest was dark all around, but Ebony knew roughly where they were. Why had the fairies abandoned her? The rain slowly stopped as the bulky man thundered through the undergrowth, dragging Ebony along with him in a vice-like grip. She had to jog to keep up with his long strides. The man stopped and Ebony almost crashed into him. He pulled something out of a pocket and turned to face her. For the first time, she got a good long look at his face. He had small, dull eyes on a wide face, and a scar ran down from his temple.

Without saying a word, he began wrapping something around Ebony's head. She squealed and tried to break free, but he swatted her hands away. A dirty cloth now obscured Ebony's vision. The man grabbed her shoulders and spun her round on the spot, then pulled her arm and continued his march.

It wasn't long before she felt quite lost—a sensation she didn't enjoy. She had always been a good navigator, and it scared her to think she didn't know which way was North. Her breath became shallow and she found herself tripping easily.

"Stop! Stop!" she shouted. The man ignored her. "Please stop. At least walk a bit slower. I can't see anything, remember?"

The man didn't reply, but he did slow down a bit, though his grip on her arm grew tighter. Ebony took a deep breath to calm her nerves and focused on her other senses. They were still in the woods. She could hear the crackle of twigs under her feet, and the smell of damp leaves surrounded them. An owl hooted from far away as a thin branch swatted at her face, making her jump. Her cheek stung in the chill wind where the branch had cut her.

They continued in this way for another mile or so, Ebony's hands growing cold and stiff.

At last, the man began to slow his pace. The air around them grew colder as they left the trees. The floor was littered with crackling leaves, but Ebony couldn't hear any snapping twigs. *We're in a glade*, she deducted.

"The other two?" said a gruff voice. There was no response, but Ebony assumed some communication had passed between them. "Ah. I'll deal with her, then," the gruff voice said.

She was passed over to another man and heard her captor walk away. Minutes later, she heard a door open, and she was shoved through. She was pushed to the back of a drafty room and tied up to a post.

The man stomped away and closed the door behind him.

"You four—don't let anyone in or out," he growled. Ebony heard the scuffing of feet approach and stop in front of the door.

The night went silent and Ebony was left blindfolded in the dark.

She was jerked awake by the sound of gruff voices outside. It took her a minute to work out why the world was so dark before remembering she was wearing a blindfold. She shook her head to try to release it, and when it didn't budge, she shook her head more roughly, but still, it wouldn't move.

She heard a scuffle from the other side of the room.

"Who's there?" she said.

No one replied, but she heard an animal huff. Maybe she was in a barn? Rubbing the back of her head on the pole behind her, the blindfold finally began to shift. It would take some effort to get it off completely, but she had all the time in the world, and she hated this endless darkness. She had no idea what time of day it was. Was it light or dark outside? It all looked the same under this rag.

It wasn't long before her scalp began to bleed. She sighed in frustration, glaring into the thick cloth. She had put herself in this position; she had to accept her circumstances. She didn't know how long it would take for Hunter to get there, if he came at all. To keep herself sane, she thought through all the questions that had been mounting in her head.

Why had Hunter cared about her so much to pay ransom for her? Why wouldn't he tell her anything? Why did he think it was too dangerous for her in the woods alone? Did he think she couldn't handle herself? With a grim chuckle, she realised she had inadvertently proved his beliefs; by getting herself caught twice, she had made herself look weak. But that didn't matter. She didn't care what he thought of her. He was untrustworthy; he was even keeping secrets from his most loyal companions. If he didn't treat his closest friends well, how did he treat others? Her instincts shouted at her to stay well away from him, but she had to know why she was so important to him. He would never leave her alone if she was a pawn in one of his games.

She shook her head to clear her mind and focused on some newer questions. What had the fairies said about a war? They had seemed reluctant to tell her. And *where* had that violence come from? Ebony knew they had some kind of magic but had never seen them use it. They had always seemed too peaceful to attack anything. But she couldn't get the image out of her mind: a hundred dark fairies, with angular, distorted, sharp faces, killing a man with lightning. It made her feel a bit sick to think they'd been capable of doing that all along. Her stomach growled and tightened into a knot. Everything she knew seemed to be turning on its head.

She'd have some answers soon. It wouldn't be long before The Foryx would try to get Bounty Hunter secrets from her. It was just a shame she didn't know any of their secrets; not enough to barter with, anyway. She'd have to use her imagination.

Sure enough, only a few hours later, she heard two pairs of boots trudging towards the barn. The doors creaked as they opened and let in a cold gust of air.

Shivering, Ebony braced herself for what might happen next.

"Let's get straight to the point, shall we?"

Ebony's head shot up and thumped into the pole behind her. She groaned and let her head droop, before remembering what had made her jump. She knew that voice. She was sure of it.

"Would it help if I took the blindfold off?"

Ebony's heart thumped and twisted. Her mind reeled. How had she got so caught up? She nodded, trying to blink away a small tear in her eye.

A hand touched her face and pulled at the blindfold. Ebony's eyes were filled with bright light. She blinked until her vision began to clear.

Standing before her, enshrouded in the light spilling from the open barn doors, was a face she had learned to trust.

Samuel Sanker.

24

She was in a barn—a large, old, run down barn. She was sat upright by the back wall opposite the closed barn doors, her hands tied with rope to a wooden beam. Her vision was blurry, covered in something sticky, and her eyes itched, but she couldn't rub them. She looked down at her lap and saw a small line of dry blood that had trickled down her top. The barn smelled of hay and horses, and before her stood Samuel Sanker. Sam. The man who had killed a Foryx to save her. The man who had kept her company for so many days and had been so kind to her.

Her head throbbed with pain and, as she rested her head against the pole behind her, she could feel a large, painful lump.

"Surprised, Ebony?" Samuel sneered. "Did you actually think I cared about you?" Ebony blushed and stared at the floor, a knot forming in her stomach.

"Nobody cares about you, Ebony. Nobody but Hunter. Do you know why that is?" Sam crouched down and stared into her face. She did her best to avoid his gaze.

"No, I don't …" Ebony mumbled.

"I didn't hear you. Speak up," Sam snapped, grabbing her chin and forcing her to look at him. Those warm eyes she had learned to trust had gone cold and hard.

"I don't know," Ebony said, enunciating every word. He stood up and towered over her. She looked up into his face. "I honestly don't know anything about him, Sam," she pleaded. He kicked her in the chest, winding the breath out of her. She coughed and wheezed as he stroked the side of her face with a finger. She gritted her teeth and forced herself to look into his eyes.

"So, you work for Everret Anders now?" she spluttered, still gasping for breath.

Sam sneered. "Anders is dead, Ebony. Keep up. I took his place months ago."

Ebony paused. Sam had probably killed him.

"Why am I here, Sam? Are you hoping Hunter will pay more ransom?"

"He won't be asked for ransom this time. I know you matter to him now. Hunter is the most respected Bounty Hunter —they hang on his every word. And we can control what he says, as long as we have you."

"He'll come for me when he works out I'm missing."

"Yes, he will … eventually. And in the meantime, I'll get some of his secrets out of you."

"I don't know any of his secrets."

Sam smiled. "We'll see about that." He put her blindfold back over her eyes, tying it uncomfortably tight, and turned to walk out of the barn. The world was dark once more.

"Why do this, Sam? He was good to you."

"There are powers stronger than Hunter Sparrow," he said, spitting out Hunter's name in disgust. "You'd do well to remember that."

As he left her, he closed the barn doors and called for some of his men to keep watch.

"Finch, tell me what happened. Where are the other two?" he asked one of the guards. Ebony assumed this must be the silent man who had dragged her through the forest.

The guard was slow to respond, taking a good minute before he replied. "They found her at a Fairy Meeting," he whispered. Ebony strained her ears to hear Sam's whispered response. "Well that's what Mace says, Sam," Finch replied under his breath. *They? Mace?* So, Sam wasn't talking to her captor? "She was right at the centre of the Meet, talking with the King and Queen. A fairy then put her to sleep. Mace and the others watched the camp for a while before going in. He only just got out with her. The other two …" Finch's sentence trailed off.

"Tell me, Finch. What is Mace saying?" Sam snapped.

Why couldn't her captor speak for himself?

"He had to leave them behind ... you said to get her out no matter what."

Sam sighed. "It's okay. I'll go back and see if I can find them—" An odd strangled cry cut him off.

"Wait, no!" Finch almost yelped, then lowered his voice. "He says not to go near the place. It was *swarming* with fairies. He—he doesn't think there's anything left of the others ..."

Sam swore under his breath. "Why do *they* care so much about her?"

"No idea. But for some reason, the damn Fae are protecting her."

The King's words rang in Ebony's ears. *We protect you and you protect us.*

"Well, that's more than we bargained for."

"What if they come here?" Finch asked, a hint of nerves in his voice.

"We run."

Since when were criminals scared of fairies? Ebony wondered. She had seen them cause some damage, but they were too peaceful to take out a whole camp of men. Were the Fae really so dangerous?

"Sam—if we keep her here, we'll be part of the war. The fairies will come for us. And Hunter won't give us any help this time."

"We'll be fine. Remember what I told you, Finch. There are powers stronger than Hunter Sparrow."

"Yes, but you still haven't explained what you mean."

"You'll see. All in good time."

"Time may not be something we have."

"Finch," Sam snapped. "We will be fine. Leave it be. And don't tell any of the other men about the damn Fae."

With that, Sam stormed off.

"He can be such an arse," Finch said out loud. "I agree, we can't fight off the fairies alone. This damn war is getting out of hand." Was he talking to Mace? Ebony couldn't hear anyone responding. And what war were they talking about? Ebony hadn't heard of any war until the fairies had mentioned it only a day ago—or was it two days ago?

"I don't know how she has managed to appease them," Finch continued. "I guess Sam will try to get that out of her, too."

Finch fell silent for a long time, leaving Ebony to her questions. It felt like many hours later that Sam returned. He burst open the barn doors, making her jump.

"Well, it seems I now need more answers from you. I need to know why the fairies are protecting you. How have you got leeway with those wasps?"

Ebony didn't reply. The fairies had been loyal to her. If he genuinely didn't know how to befriend them, she wasn't going to say a thing. She needed to distract him with other answers—even if they were made up.

"I've never seen the fairies act like that." Ebony said, turning her head to look at him—at least, she thought she was looking at him. She couldn't see anything through the blindfold.

"That's not an answer." Ebony felt him grip her arm. "Why are they protecting you?" His grip tightened.

"Why don't the Fae like you? You managed to charm *me*—fairies can't be that difficult."

"Don't act so naive. You know those critters are the most dangerous creatures in the forest. I expect Hunter told you all about our war with them when he was at your camp."

He didn't tell me anything, Ebony thought begrudgingly.

Ebony shrugged. "They always seemed harmless to me."

"They don't like Outlaws. They think the forest belongs to them. Any of this ringing a bell?"

"Well maybe it *should* belong to them. The Fae were here first."

"You can't just *appease* them. No—you know something. They don't just tolerate you; they protect you. Why?"

When Ebony didn't reply, she received a harsh punch to her jaw. She longed to cradle her face in her hands, but they were growing numb strapped behind her back.

"I don't know why! And I don't know anything about any war. Apparently, I'm even more ignorant than you." That remark received a stinging slap.

Sam sighed. "The Fae don't like us outlaws. They've been trying to fight us for years. They sabotage plans, destroy camps ... but recently it has got much worse. They have begun attacking us and we have no way of fighting back." He lowered his head, as if ashamed at this weakness. "That's where you come in. You can help us beat them."

Ebony chuckled, which seemed to anger Sam. "You can't beat them. They're some of the oldest creatures in the world. They have knowledge we could hardly fathom. They tolerate me because I live alongside them, not against them. But I still don't know why they want to protect me." She paused, then mumbled, "I'm not surprised they hate *you*." Sam kicked her knee and a sharp jabbing pain shot up her leg. Ebony heard his feet retreating and the barn door close roughly behind him.

25

In the far corner of the barn, about fifty feet from Ebony, she could hear a horse kicking at the dry, muddy ground and chewing on a large pile of hay, paying her no mind.

She needed an escape plan. No one was looking for her; no one knew where she was or even that she was in danger. And she doubted anyone would even care. Even the fairies had let her down. Why weren't they protecting her like they had promised?

She sat in silence for what felt like hours, listening to the horse snort and grunt and endlessly chew at hay.

The next time Sam visited her, he was in a better mood. Ebony didn't know how much time had passed. Her blindfold would not budge, so she couldn't tell day from night. The barn door opened slowly, making Ebony shiver.

"I have to see your face when I show you this," Sam said from the entrance. Ebony could hear a smile in his words. With a light tread, he made his way to her and took off her blindfold. It was growing dark outside, but Sam held a lantern that gleamed before her. The relief of being able to see again took over for a moment before she remembered that Sam was before her, grinning like an idiot.

"I have some news—something to tell you," he said, like a child with a secret. "Something you should have known a long time ago." He crouched down and leaned towards her. Lowering his voice, he said, "I know why Hunter cares about you. I know why you're so important to him." Ebony gave him a quizzical look. "I've suspected for a while, actually. But now I have *proof* of his biggest secret." He paused, smiling at her look of bewilderment. "You really don't know, do you?"

"Don't know what?" Ebony grumbled as her stomach gave a pang of hunger.

"You don't know who he is …"

"What do you mean? He's Hunter Sparrow, the Bounty Hunter we'd both wish was dead."

Sam gave an over-exaggerated look of shock. "That's not a very nice thing to say about your uncle."

Ebony paused, trying to understand what he had just said. "What do you mean? What are you on about?"

"You heard me. Hunter Sparrow is your uncle."

"I don't have any family, Sam. I grew up in the Clink."

"He's been lying to you. He left you there when your parents died. He left you with the – what do you call them? The Snatchers." Sam had a look somewhere between amusement and anger.

Ebony's stomach twisted. It *did* make sense. It answered a lot of questions. But if it was true—a fact Ebony was truly struggling to believe—why had he suddenly started caring about her now after sixteen years?

"So, where's your proof?" she snapped.

He produced a thin, white sheet of paper from a pocket and handed it to Ebony. She had never been very good at reading. Most of the words on the page looked like an odd jumble of letters that she vaguely remembered learning when she was little.

Seeing her nonplussed expression, Sam took back the paper and read it to her.

"Registration District of birth: Port, East Dwellings—Male, born 'Huntington Sparrow Wick', born in Summer 864—father was 'Alistair Wick', mother was 'Ada Robin Rowe'. One sibling, male." He paused. "So, that makes him … thirty-two years old." He looked triumphant. Ebony didn't respond. She couldn't find the words. "Well? Isn't his birth certificate enough proof? 'Wick' isn't exactly a common name."

Her mind fell silent as it all fell into place. Her family had come from the East Dwellings—they must have had money once. She had never been told how her parents had died. She had just been delivered to an orphanage as a baby by a stranger—a man, the matron had always said, who had known no more about Ebony's family than anyone else. If Hunter really was her uncle, then he'd be able to tell her something—*anything*—about her parents. He clearly cared for family, even if he *had* abandoned her as a child. He must have been only sixteen or seventeen. She could have lived with him in the forest all her life, but instead she'd endured the orphanages of the Commons ... and that fire... the fire that had changed everything. Her eyes stung with tears—of anger, discovery, sadness, loss ... her mind reeled.

"You know, we're not so different, you and I," Sam said after a long silence.

Ebony snapped out of her reverie.

"We are *nothing* alike," she spat. "I am a Dweller, you are a *Human*."

Sam almost looked hurt. "I'm not a Human. I don't belong with them—I never did. I'm different to them."

"No, you're not," Ebony replied, glaring at him, her eyes blurred with tears. "You're one of the worst Humans."

Sam laughed. "You haven't met any other Humans. You know nothing of the worst Humans. Besides, I am much better than a Human—because I have *Him* on my side."

Ebony ignored him. She wasn't in the mood for riddles.

"He elevates me—He makes me stronger and wiser."

Ebony sighed and gave him what we wanted. "Who? Who elevates you?"

Sam smiled, a darkness in his eyes.

"The Shadow."

Ebony laughed. He honestly believed she would fall for that?

"What's so funny?" Sam asked, irritated that his threat hadn't scared her.

"The Shadow isn't real, Sam."

He gave her a quizzical look. "Yes, it is. I've seen it; spoken with it."

"Of course you have. *I'm* the Shadow!" she laughed.

Sam glared at her. His expression began to soften as realisation hit, but he never took his eyes off her. He smiled, with a dark sparkle in his eyes.

"So, you're the Demon they talk about?"

Ebony didn't reply, just smirked at him. She hadn't expected him to be so gullible.

"I don't mean *that* Shadow. I mean the real one," he said.

Ebony's smile slipped. "What do you mean?"

It was Sam's turn to smirk. "All stories have an element of truth behind them."

"What is that supposed to mean?" she asked, bewildered. Was there another person like her out there?

"You must have heard the stories. The Shadow, cursed by darkness with claws and sharp teeth; the child taken by the Shadowlands; the Fae flee before it …"

Ebony scoffed, then paused. Was that what the fairies had seen in the trees? Was that why they hadn't followed her when she was being dragged away from her camp?

"How did you kill all of Bates' men? And why did you help me kill Bates?"

"I wanted to gain your trust. But that proved too difficult."

You did gain my trust, Ebony thought to herself, shame flooding through her for being so gullible. Had he purposefully only answered one of her questions?

"I think I'll leave this with you," he said, folding up the birth certificate and tucking it into Ebony's trouser pocket. He then left the barn, forgetting to put Ebony's blindfold back on.

She felt deflated. She had always been alone. She had always had to fight alone; for herself, her own safety, her own health. And all this time, she'd had family, alive and well. And Hunter had known about her all along. In that moment, she felt the exhaustion of her sixteen years of survival weigh on her shoulders, which slumped. What kind of man abandoned his dead brother's baby? Something inside her twisted in anger.

She shook her head. She still didn't have concrete proof—not until he admitted it. But if it was true, she needed to know more. Did she have any other family members still alive? How did her parents die? Why had Hunter taken her to the Snatchers? Why had he lied to her the last few weeks? And why only now did he care for her safety?

Her dreams while in that barn were full of images; none of which added up or made much sense.

A small boy fed cookies to Hunter, who laughed at Ebony while she watched, tied up to a pole. They sat around the fire in her camp and Ebony sat whittling arrows, Sam beside her. Hunter hugged her, then cackled wickedly and stole her arrows from her.

"Hey! Give that back!" Ebony shouted.

Hunter laughed again and then fired the arrows into a tree. They all broke and fell to the ground in pieces.

"Why did you do that?" she asked him, as if he had just killed someone she loved.

"Because I'm your Uncle," Hunter replied.

"No, you're not." Ebony said. "I've got no one. All my family are dead."

The clearing was suddenly clear, except for Hunter who stood before her with an odd expression. "Your family aren't dead. They just didn't want you."

Ebony lost track of how many times she had this dream. Sometimes they weren't in her camp; sometimes they were in Hunter's tent and sometimes in this very barn. But the characters remained the same.

26

Ebony's neck was aching and her eyes blinked in the sunlight that flooded into the room. There must have been a window somewhere above her. It was easier to count the time passing now that her blindfold had come off. Sam hadn't returned and nobody had provided any food. A guard would enter the barn every few hours, tilt her head back, and pour some water down her throat. So, they definitely wanted to keep her alive. Her hands were almost numb and the rope around her wrists had begun to dig into her skin, making it red and sore. Ebony felt dizzy and nauseous from the lack of food. She had tried asking a guard for something to eat, but he had thumped her head on the wooden pole behind her, making the world go dark. She had a bruise forming on the back of her head, and she was sure Sam had given her a black eye. Her right eye felt swollen and heavy. At night, the room was so dark, she strained to see anything at all. The night air had grown so chilly, she felt her lips turning blue. As the sun came up, the barn would warm up slightly, but not enough.

She knew she wouldn't survive much longer like this. She had grown so weak, she didn't know if she would be able to stand. It was tiring just lifting her head. Her mind instinctively listened to every sound of movement from outside, keeping her from sleeping. What was she listening for? She started to wonder if she had made a serious mistake. Was Hunter going to come for her or did he really not care? Even if Sam was right about Hunter's lineage, that didn't necessarily mean he would rescue Ebony. Sam must know that. He was keeping her alive *in case* Hunter tried to rescue her—but why? To prove a point? To spill his secret? If he didn't rescue her—well, Sam would have to decide how long to wait until his trap had failed. Ebony doubted Sam would keep her alive if he had been wrong about Hunter's family ties.

But what would Sam get out of it all? It took a while for Ebony to realise that all he wanted was the secret. These outlaws didn't only hunt people and objects; they hunted knowledge. They knew that knowledge was more dangerous.

If Hunter had only just started caring about Ebony, then he almost certainly needed her for one of his plans. She was definitely a pawn in one of his games. Despite her anger at Hunter for abandoning her and then lying to her, Ebony knew there was only one way to get all the answers she needed. She would have to get closer to Hunter. She needed to let him think that his plan was working—whatever the plan was.

The night was drawing in. The horse lay down on a pile of straw and huffed, clearly unhappy in the cold night air. A small sliver of light from the doorway was slowly disappearing. Ebony prepared herself for another long night of no sleep and endless cold. Hours later, Ebony was resting her head on the wooden pole she was tied to, doing her best to doze. A twig snapped in the woods and she jerked awake. She sighed. It was probably just an animal, like it had been all the other nights.

She leaned her head back and tried to doze again. But then she heard something else. A loud voice shouting. It was too far away to make out any words, but it definitely had an element of fear to it.

She began to smell smoke.

More voices started to shout now. A cacophony of frightened yells surrounded the barn, though all were still too far away to hear any words. Then she heard a clanging sound, like the ring of steel on steel. Someone was swordfighting.

"He's here. They're here," Sam's voice called from outside, making her jump. Through the barn doors, Ebony could see the camp before her—ablaze. Her heart started to race. She was trapped in a wooden barn, surrounded by burning buildings.

"Let me go, Sam! Please," she begged. He was standing in the doorway now, holding a sword, his figure silhouetted against the flames. "We'll burn in here!"

"No, we won't. He'll get here before then."

"If he's here, then he's already proved that he cares about me—he's proved his lineage ..." Ebony wasn't sure she believed her own words, but she had to get through to Sam somehow. "His secret is out. So you can let me go now."

"No, I can't. He needs to come here first."

Ebony got the feeling that Sam hadn't told her everything—there was more to his plan. Had he laid a trap for Hunter?

Ebony heard heavy boots thundering towards the barn and saw Sam brace himself. It sounded like there were about five men charging at him. But he didn't move. Why didn't he move?

Then she heard screams. The men were being massacred—but how? By what? Was this how Sam had killed Bates' men? Sam stood stock still, watching what must have been a gruesome scene play out before him. Silence fell. Ebony glanced around the barn, expecting to see smoke. The horse had begun whinnying and kicking at the ground—and there was something behind it. Something that hadn't been there before. There was a figure standing by the horse. It looked like a shadow with a form—a shadow with red eyes. It stood and watched her, hardly noticing the panicking horse. Ebony hardly dared breathe but couldn't tear her eyes from the shape in the darkness. The barn felt still, and goosebumps raced up her arms. There was something unearthly about the figure—something darker than night.

A noise from the barn door made her jump. She saw Sam stride out into the night, toward the fires. When she looked back at the horse, the dark figure was gone. She couldn't decide if she had imagined it or not. Perhaps her mind was playing tricks on her? She hadn't eaten or slept in days. She must have imagined it.

The smell of smoke grew stronger. To her horror, she could see smoke in the far corner to her right. Her heart began to race. It didn't take long for the barn to catch fire. The flames licked up the walls surprisingly fast. Her worst fear was coming true. But last time, she had been free to escape. This time, she was tied to a wooden pole in a building made of wood. She redoubled her attempts to break free, but the rope around her wrists wouldn't budge.

"Help!" she cried. Smoke had begun to fill the room and burned her throat as she inhaled. "Help!" she croaked. Her voice was already cracking. With all the energy she had left, she tried her best to break the ropes or wriggle her fingers out of them, rubbing them against the wood and hoping the rope would fray, but to no avail. All she achieved was some sharp, painful splinters in her hands.

She began to cry out, yelling as loud as she could, tears forming in her eyes and blurring her vision. She wasn't sure if she was crying or if the smoke was making her eyes water. She couldn't see the barn doors anymore and the room was growing hotter by the minute. She soon found she could no longer cry out without coughing. Panic began to rise in her chest. Her nightmare flashed before her eyes—her memories coming back to haunt her.

A dorm room, thick with smoke and flames. A small boy crying out for help. She was running through the corridors of the orphanage trying to find her best friend. Henry. Where was Henry? He always snuck down to the kitchens at night to steal cookies. Her fist was clenched around the hilt of Henry's dagger; the one his father had given him before he'd died. He'd managed to keep it secret for years. Of all things, Henry would want to save that knife from a burning building. She skidded around a corner as the roof crumpled behind her. Perhaps he was outside already? She raced down the stairs, fire licking the walls all around her, the smoke so dense she couldn't see more than a few steps ahead. At last, she found the front doors of the orphanage and burst out. There was a crowd outside, watching the building crumble from within.

Gasping for air, ten-year-old Ebony cried out for her best friend, but he never answered. With one last crash, the building completely collapsed in on itself.

"Henry! Henry!" she called. But he was nowhere to be seen.

She could swear she could see Henry before her as the barn became thick with smoke. A small boy still, only eight years old, grinned at her, then disappeared.

Tears filled her eyes and she felt her heart break all over again. They had been a team. They had survived The Clink together. But she had lost him, just like she had lost her family. He had been taken by the flames, no trace to be found.

The barn was unbearably hot now and beginning to crumble. Ebony's eyes began to close, and her head grew heavy. She heard something approach her, but nothing seemed to make sense anymore.

"Henry," she croaked quietly and let out a sob.

The barn door was open and above her loomed three men, silhouetted in red hot flames, their faces dirty with soot and ash. Someone began untying her hands. She vaguely recognised their faces in the dark. Beside her, Darrel was fiddling with the tight ropes in the darkness. In front of her stood Halsey and Lennox. The last time she had seen these people, she'd had to hide from them because of the spreading rumours about her and Hunter. So why were they here now, rescuing her?

"Where is she?" said a voice from the barn entrance, its owner obscured.

Ebony's chest filled with a mixture of relief, anger, and nerves. She didn't want to face him yet—not now, not in this state.

Hunter strode past the other three and crouched down in front of her.

"You're safe now," Ebony. "We're here."

Looking into his grubby face, his ginger hair falling loose from its ponytail, Ebony felt a tear fall down her cheek—was it a tear of joy and relief or a tear of sorrow and anger? She couldn't tell.

"Do you think you can walk?" Hunter asked her.

Ebony slowly shook her head.

"Let's get her standing, lads." Hunter said.

Darrel and Halsey took an arm each and hauled her to her feet. Almost instantly, her knees buckled. Hunter caught her before she hit the ground. She put all her weight into him, her head so dizzy, the room was spinning.

"I think we're going to need to carry her," Lennox suggested.

Hunter leaned down and lifted her up into his arms as if she was light as a feather.

"Lead the way, lads. We need to get out of here. Whatever killed the others will be after us soon."

The others? Ebony vaguely recalled the screeching sounds from earlier. *They had all been Bounty Hunters? They all came for me?* She shook her head, hardly noticing the odd look Lennox gave her. *No. They came because Hunter told them to*, she reasoned with herself.

With one last look back at the blazing camp, Sam nowhere to be seen, Darrel, Halsey, and Lennox led Hunter back through the forest, Ebony cradled in his arms.

27

Ebony's right eye wouldn't open. It was so swollen, it hurt to blink. She opened her other eye and found herself in an unnervingly familiar room filled with empty crates. She lay tangled in a warm fur blanket on a pile of pillows in the corner of the room. She felt hot and sweaty and moved a heavy, swollen arm out from under the covers. In fact, her whole body felt swollen, but not as painful as her eye. She was lying on her back, staring at a canvas ceiling she knew only too well. Her heart sank. Had she dreamed her escape from the Bounty Hunters' camp? Had she ever gone home at all? Movement came from the entrance to the tent and she tried to sit up to see who it was, but it felt like something was pulling her back down, like she was glued to the pillows she lay on.

A middle-aged blonde lady approached with a tray of colourful liquids. Ebony recognised the Carer. She tried to sit up again, but the lady pushed her shoulder back down to the ground and Ebony willingly obeyed. She felt like something was sitting on her chest.

She broke out in a fit of coughing, curling into a tight ball under the covers. As she coughed, breathed, swallowed, she felt searing pain down her throat and grimaced.

"You need to sleep, dear," the blonde woman said. She handed Ebony a small ceramic mug of water and pushed Ebony's back into a seating position, allowing Ebony to rest on the woman's hand. "Take small sips."

Ebony couldn't manage more than a sip at a time. Her hands shook as she held the mug—it seemed heavier than it looked. Once she had drunk all the water, the woman handed her another mug of green, mushy liquid.

"This is a blend of herbs that will nourish you back to health. You haven't eaten for a while and it will take your body time to get used to food again."

Ebony drank it without questioning what was in it. She had to chew on some soggy, bitter leaves before the woman would take the drink away from her. In a third mug was a hot drink, its warmth inviting Ebony's cold, clammy hands.

"Wassit?" Ebony managed to croak, wincing at the pain in her throat as she spoke.

"Don't try to talk, dear."

Ebony looked at her imploringly, as if to say, *What can I do?*

The woman's expression replied, *not much.*

Ebony looked at the drink quizzically and sniffed it. It smelled powerful—almost alcoholic.

"Some call it a hot toddy. Hot water, sugar, and a dash of whisky. Heals a fever in no time."

Ebony accepted the beverage and savoured its warmth as she drank. The whisky quickly began to make her feel drowsy and even heavier than before. The woman laid her back down again and tucked the blanket in around her.

Ebony couldn't remember the last time she had felt so cosy.

When she woke up, Hunter was sitting on the chair where Sam had sat for so many hours. A pang of pain shot through her chest. She had been so stupid, thinking she could trust someone. Hunter had his eyes closed and was snoring quietly. How long had he been sitting there? Ebony tried to sit up to see if he was really asleep but doubled up in another painful coughing fit. Hunter sat bolt upright, took one look at her, and immediately left the tent. At first, Ebony assumed this was because he didn't want her to know that he had been sitting there, watching over her. But only minutes later, a familiar face appeared, a panicking Hunter by her side. He fidgeted with his hands, his shirt, his ginger ponytail, which was messier than usual, his face etched with worry. Using her one good eye, Ebony thought he looked paler and older.

"Is she going to be okay, Daya?" Hunter asked.

Daya sighed. "How many times are you going to ask me that?"

"Until you know for sure that she will be okay."

Since when did Hunter care so much for my health? Ebony wondered. *And why is Daya looking after me? I thought she didn't like me?*

"I told you. It will take time, but I'm pretty sure she will be okay."

"Only pretty sure?"

"Hunter, I will not repeat myself again," Daya snapped.

Hunter backed down and sat on his chair, looking miserable.

Daya knelt down beside Ebony. "Do you think you could try to say something for me?"

Ebony looked into her blue, caring eyes. She had never met someone like this—someone who honestly seemed to care for someone else's health, willing and able to push personal issues to one side to do her job.

Ebony croaked something inaudible. Her throat was less sore, but it was still difficult to speak.

Hunter was peering over at them, as if convinced Daya was giving Ebony either poison or a miracle cure. Daya turned to him with a look of amusement.

"Give her another day, Hunter. Try talking to her tomorrow."

A lone tear rolled down Ebony's eye, knowing that she would have a while before she could walk properly, let alone talk. Daya wiped the tear from her cheek and gave her a warm smile.

"You'll be okay, dear. Just give it time. I'll get you another hot toddy."

Ebony felt more tears cloud her eyes. But these weren't tears of sorrow or self-pity. She was crying because she was being looked after. Wasn't that a happy thing? Shouldn't she be smiling? Daya appeared to have forgiven her, or had begun tolerating her existence, at least. The more she questioned her tears, the more tears came. She reached out a hand and touched Daya's arm.

"It's no problem, dear. This is my job in this camp. I'm a Carer."

But whether she knew it or not, Daya was healing more than just an illness.

It took another two days before Ebony could speak again. Hunter had spent most of his time in the chair, hurrying out for Daya's aid every time Ebony coughed, sneezed, or groaned. Daya kept Ebony dosed up on any medicines she could muster.

"Hunter," Ebony managed to croak one day. He rushed to her side.

"What can I get you? Do you need Daya?" He spoke so fast, Ebony had to concentrate to understand what he was saying.

"No, no—" she croaked. "Hunter?" she said.

"Yes, Eb?"

She was too tired to reprimand him for calling her Eb, so she ignored it.

"What happened?"

"What happened when?"

"The Foryx—fire."

Hunter looked taken aback, as if he had only just realised that she didn't know the full story.

"Oh—um. We rescued you."

Ebony huffed. "I know. But how?"

Hunter sighed then pulled his chair over to her side and sat down.

"We set the place on fire."

"Why?"

"No one captures my people and gets away with it."

Everything Sam had told her about Hunter flashed through her mind. Was it true or had Sam made it up? He had been the one to read the document, after all.

"But—why fire?"

"We needed a distraction," Hunter shrugged.

"Why—" Ebony coughed. "Why did you come for me?"

"You're one of us," Hunter replied. But there was something about this reply that felt practised. Or maybe she was just imagining it.

"I'm not—I broke the rules, left, ran away … Why did your people rescue me?" Ebony started a coughing fit again. Just as Hunter was ready to fetch Daya, Ebony waved at him as if to say she didn't need help. She looked at him, waiting for his answer.

"Because I told them to."

Ebony had expected as much.

"But why—" she coughed. "Why did you tell them to?" By this point, talking was starting to hurt again, like sandpaper on her throat.

Hunter paused, calculating his response. "I told you—I want you to join us. You'd be a good asset. Can't have you join us if you're dead."

This reply definitely sounded practiced, like he was using excuses that he had told himself so often, they had almost become true. With an odd sinking feeling, mixed with intrigue and a hint of anger, Ebony suspected that she knew the truth. But she was too tired now to bring it all up with him. Besides, she'd rather she had a voice when she tackled that subject.

"Eb, we burnt down their entire camp." He paused. "Do you know what this means?" Ebony gave him a quizzical look. "It means we're at war with The Foryx Clan."

Ebony took a moment to let this sink in. What exactly would war entail?

"Will they hurt us?"

"They may try to. But they're too weak now. It will take them a while to get their strength back. But The Foryx will take their revenge, especially with Sam leading them."

Ebony tried not to think about Sam. His betrayal had hurt her more than she wanted to admit.

"Why are you rivals?" Ebony said in a raspy whisper.

"It's a long story involving betrayal of trust and secrets. A man called Mace once thought he could do better than me."

"Better? At what?"

"At creating a team of Bounty Hunters." Ebony took a minute to understand what he meant, but he clarified for her. "They're not as good as us. Don't have the brain, only the brawn." He stopped to think. "We've been coexisting quite well for a few years now. But then they discovered you—and Sam ..." His voice filled with pain. "I don't know how he fooled me so easily. I trusted a Human! I can't believe I was so stupid." He shook his head slowly in disbelief.

"We both were," Ebony whispered. "I thought he was my friend. But I don't have friends. I should have remembered that."

"I'm your friend," Hunter replied.

Ebony couldn't stop a chuckle leaving her chest but managed to disguise it as a cough. She didn't know *what* he was. He was either anything but a friend or so much more than just a friend. Somehow, despite the fact that he had rescued her, he was both.

Her eyes began to feel heavy and Hunter stood up. "I'll leave you to sleep," he said.

"Wait," Ebony croaked, wincing as pain seared her throat. "I'll join you," she whispered. "I'll join the Bounty Hunters. For real this time."

Hunter's eyebrows rose. "Why the change of heart?"

"I owe those men—the ones who died trying to rescue me. And—" she paused, unsure whether she should finish her sentence. But if she was to earn his trust, he had to think she needed him. "I can't get revenge on Samuel Sanker on my own," she said, spitting out his name.

Hunter nodded. "Neither can I."

They stared into each other's eyes for a long heartbeat, reading each other's humiliation and anger at being wrong-footed and betrayed.

"Eb, how did those men die?" Hunter asked.

Ebony thought back, trying to decipher the blur of the last few hours in that godforsaken barn.

"I don't know ... I just heard ... screeching, wailing. They were massacred. I thought *you* would know," she said with a raspy voice.

Hunter shook his head and frowned.

"Hunter?" It was Ebony's turn to ask a question. "Are you going to keep me in here again?"

He smiled. "No—you're free to go as you please. I clearly can't control you, and you'd find a way to escape, anyway. Besides, I'm going to need you to fight when you're back to strength." He looked away from her and stared out of the entrance of the tent. "But for now, you're confined to that bed. I want you back to health as soon as possible. Besides, you might have got out of my clutches, but good luck getting out of Daya's." He smiled mischievously. He looked a lot happier now that Ebony was showing signs of health again.

"I'll check in on you later, Eb," he said before strolling out of the tent.

28

It took about a week for Daya to allow Ebony out of her bed to get some fresh air. She breathed in the fresh, winter breeze and the damp smell of fallen leaves. Hunter's tent wasn't far from her own. For the first time in many days, she stretched her legs, making her way towards Hunter, who was standing by his wooden table with a few other men. As she approached, Hunter raised his eyes and beamed.

"Join us!" he called to her.

Ebony tentatively approached the table to find an odd assortment of objects and little clay balls that looked randomly placed but must have had some kind of design.

"How are you?" one of the Hunters asked her. She struggled to recall his name.

Ebony shrugged. "I can stand," she said, feeling shy.

"Always a bonus," Hunter replied. "Tell us what you think of our battle strategy," he said, pointing at the table.

"Is this your plan to get back at The Foryx?" Ebony asked.

"Oh—no. We need to get past the fairies first … I haven't been able to tell you much about it yet …"

Ebony felt a knot form in her stomach. She couldn't possibly help Hunter fight the fairies—they were her only true allies; the only people she could trust.

"Not really up to much thinking yet …" she mumbled, and went to sit in a chair in the corner of the tent, hugging her knees to her chest.

Hunter looked from her to his men and dismissed them, suggesting they finish their plans tomorrow.

"What's up, Eb?" Hunter asked, bringing a chair to sit next to her.

"What do you mean?" Ebony replied, staring at the floor.

"You're not being your normal self. No strong opinions, no quips …"

Ebony took her time to reply.

"I guess … I'm just a bit confused."

"Confused? About what?"

"Everything."

"Ebony, I can't read your mind."

Ebony looked up at him and sighed. "I always thought I could do everything alone. But I think, without Daya, I would probably have died." *And that would have been my fault entirely*, Ebony thought. She had got herself captured on purpose, after all.

Hunter nodded. "She's our best healer."

"I owe a lot to her."

"No, you don't. Just because someone helped you, that doesn't mean you owe them."

Ebony didn't reply. They sat in silence for a few minutes before Hunter spoke.

"What did Sam say to you while he had you in that barn? Anything we can use to fight him?"

Ebony sighed with exasperation. Would he ever tell her the truth?

"He said something—I kind of ignored him at the time. But I can't get it out of my head now," she replied.

"What did he say?"

"He said something about a shadow—*The* Shadow. He had The Shadow on his side … and he didn't mean my nickname, either." Hunter's face had turned ashen.

"Just before the camp set on fire … I saw something. Or, I think I did. I'm not sure if I imagined it or not …"

"A dark figure in the corner of the room staring at you?"

Ebony froze. How could he possibly have known what she had seen? He replied before she could ask.

"I've seen it before. I've heard of The Shadow before."

"It's real?" Ebony had seen the dark figure in her dreams every night for the past week.

"Well—maybe we both imagined it?"

They looked at each other in apprehension. Ebony couldn't help but notice a look of dread in Hunter's eyes.

"Why does it scare you?" she asked.

"It doesn't scare me," Hunter said, getting up from his seat and pacing. "It's just a story. I doubt it's real."

His sudden change of tack told her he was hiding something from her.

"But you know something about it, don't you?"

"It doesn't matter now. I'm sure Sam was bluffing—"

"No!" Ebony said firmly, surprising herself. "You're not doing that to me anymore."

"Doing what?"

"Keeping secrets from me."

"What do you mean?"

Ebony paused. It was time to let him know what she knew.

"I know why you were keeping me guarded. Sam told me."

"What did Sam tell you? You can't trust a word he says."

"He showed me your birth certificate. Is it true? Are you my Uncle?" Hunter froze and turned away from her. "Well? Are you?"

He looked over his shoulder at her. "You weren't supposed to find out."

Ebony's head swam, her chest tightened, her heart was beat fast. It was true. She had so many questions she hardly knew where to start.

"Why didn't you tell me?" she blurted out, outraged.

"You're safer not knowing—not caring about me."

"What is *that* supposed to mean?"

"I trade in secrets, Ebony. That means my secrets are always in danger. *You* are my secret."

"But why? Why did you abandon me to the Snatchers? I grew up in hell because of you! I survived a burning orphanage, I lost my best friend, I became an outlaw when I was a child and lived alone in the woods for two years!"

"I thought you liked living alone?"

"Everyone I have ever known has abandoned me. My parents, my best friend, and my father's brother—my Uncle."

"Your parents didn't abandon you. They died trying to save you."

"From what?"

"I—I don't know. I was hoping you did. That's why I came to find you. And then I saw how good you were at surviving and I realised you were only that good because I left you in that orphanage."

Ebony's eyes were blurry with tears of pain, anger, longing. She had given up learning about her parents long ago—before the fire had driven her into the forest.

"I don't have a family because of you. This place—the Bounty Hunters—they could have been my family if you hadn't abandoned me."

"We're your family, *now*."

Ebony looked away from him and gazed into the clearing outside.

"How did you know where I was? When you rescued me, I mean."

"When you disappeared, I figured you had gone back to your camp. So, I went to find you, but you were nowhere to be seen. But when I saw the two bodies, it was obvious what had happened."

"But you took days to come to my camp. What took you so long?"

Hunter shook his head slowly and let out a sigh. "I was needed elsewhere. I've also been trying to protect my niece—your cousin. Her parents died a few weeks ago, so I hid her at a friend's place in town."

I have a cousin? So that explained the girl Ebony had seen him with in town.

"So, your brother—or sister?—died a few weeks ago?" Ebony asked, her eyes wide.

"Well, he was my half-brother. To be honest, I hardly knew him. But I'm convinced he didn't die of 'natural causes' as they claim. Someone is knocking off my family members and I don't know why." He frowned.

"I've got a deal for you," Ebony said, trying to keep her voice steady. She looked at him again, her yellow eyes more determined than before. "I will join the Bounty Hunters if you tell me everything you know about my parents and their deaths."

"I know very little about their deaths."

"You'll tell me everything you *do* know about them, and as you find out more, you'll tell me that, too. And I'll help you find out about your half-brother. I can give you Tusting Hicks as an ally—though convincing him might be a struggle." Ebony was on a roll now. Before Hunter could answer her demands, she continued, "And I get to have my own tent—I'm not staying in the barracks. If you don't agree, I'll disappear, and I won't keep your secret safe. Those are my conditions."

Hunter looked at her, his eyebrows raised with a look of amusement.

"The secret is out now. I had to tell some of the men to persuade them to help me rescue you."

"Who knows?"

"Darrel, Halsey, Lennox, and Daya."

So that's why Daya isn't jealous anymore, Ebony reasoned.

"They won't betray your secrets, though. They respect you too much."

"And you will?"

Ebony shrugged. "If I have reason to."

Hunter gave her a grim look. "Fine. It's a deal. But you have to learn to work in a team."

"I get to *lead* a team," Ebony added.

"Maybe one day."

Ebony sighed and thought it all through. She would be warm for the winter, she could still continue looting with Tusting, she'd have food that she didn't have to hunt for … and she would be able to find out more about her parents and family.

"Deal," she said. Hunter and Ebony shook hands.

"So, tell me about my parents." Ebony said.

Hunter sighed. "I won't tell you everything now. You're going to learn to work in a team first."

Ebony looked at him expectantly. Anything was better than nothing.

"You know your blue ring?" He said.

"The one you stole from me, you mean?"

"Well—the one I borrowed …"

"What about it?

"It was your mother's. I'm pretty sure it was the same one she used to wear."

Ebony's jaw dropped. "But how did I just *happen* to find it?"

"Fluke? I don't know," Hunter said, slowly shaking his head in disbelief. He paused, considering if he should say more. "You know I said I'd seen colour-changing eyes before?" Hunter began. Ebony nodded. "They were your mother's, too. I never found out why her eyes changed. I don't even know if *she* knew why."

Ebony's vision started to spin slightly. It was almost as if the world had started falling into place all around her. She quickly sat down on a stool in the corner of the tent.

"What was her name?" Ebony asked, looking up at him.

"Terra."

"What was my father's name?"

"Michael."

"How did they die?"

Hunter paused, then said slowly, "They were attacked. I don't know why, yet, or who did it."

Ebony fell silent. She looked to the floor and shuffled her feet. Maybe she wasn't as ready as she had thought.

"I need to get the stuff from my den …" she said suddenly and left the tent.

An hour later, she was making her way through the forest towards her den, preparing herself to say goodbye to her favourite clearing in Rundlewood Forest. It appeared through the trees, looking lonely. The den was still intact. Sam knew where this camp was now, so she kept herself vigilant, weapons at the ready.

She dismantled her fireplace, which had made a dark burn stain on the forest floor. Various logs sat around the fire, acting as seats. She threw these into the forest before collecting the few things she hadn't given to Tusting for safekeeping, including her dagger that was still lying in her den. She'd have to rescue the bags he had stowed another time.

She took down her den last, her heart feeling heavy. Life as she knew it was about to change drastically. There would be no more quiet mornings, no more visiting fairies, no more traps to set for meat. She didn't know if she was relieved or not. Before leaving, she covered her tracks and then sat down on the forest floor where the fire had once been.

"Coralia?" Ebony said quietly, then said the name again more loudly, calling out into the trees. "Queen Coralia? King Alvero?" There was no response. The trees stood still and Ebony sighed. Perhaps the fairies had grown tired of looking after her when she had willingly handed herself over? She lowered her head and began picking at frosted leaves on the ground.

She heard a light buzzing sound in the trees but thought nothing of it. It soon grew louder, and she looked up to see a swarm of fairies headed towards her camp, all wanting to speak to her.

The fairies surrounded her in a circle, just as they had done before, though there weren't quite as many now. Before her hovered one fairy; Queen Coralia.

"We are glad to see you alive, Ebony Wick."

Ebony smiled. "Thank you, your Majesty. I'm sorry I had to put you through that. I wanted to be captured to get some answers."

"Did you get them?" Coralia asked in her quiet voice.

"Some of them. But I need more answers, and I only have one way of getting them. And you're not going to like it."

The Queen's buzzing fell silent, waiting for Ebony to elaborate.

"The leader of the Bounty Hunters is my Uncle. I only just found out. He can tell me more about my family and how they died. But he'll only tell me if I join the Bounty Hunters."

"Wicked," Coralia said. "Cold hearts."

"I know. They're not good people. They're liars and cheats. But I have to know how my parents died—and I need to know more about me and where I came from."

"We understand," the fairies chorused, then fell silent.

"Would you tell me about this war with them?" Ebony asked.

"Hunters invade our land. They do not respect the forest. You live *with* us. They live *against* us," she said slowly.

Ebony frowned. "Perhaps I can help? I can spy for you—get information on their war. I could try to teach them how to live *with* you, but I don't know if they'll listen."

The fairies didn't reply.

"This isn't a safe place anymore, your Majesty. Samuel Sanker knows this place, and he is not a good person. He said he has The Shadow on his side. Do you know what that means?" Ebony asked in earnest.

A shudder moved through the crowd of fairies.

"A great evil. We all hide our shadows; he does not," she said at last.

"What do you mean?"

"Our inner shadows. Our darkest core." Coralia said, touching her heart. "We bury it. He does not."

Ebony gazed round at the fairies, who had all become agitated.

"We must leave here now. We will meet again, Ebony Wick," Queen Coralia said. And with that, all of the fairies flew away into the trees, leaving the clearing quiet and still once again.

With one last glance around the clearing, Ebony hoisted her bag onto her back and began the walk towards her future. Towards the Bounty Hunters.

MADDY GLENN grew up in rural Sussex, England, and knew she wanted to be an author from a young age. Excelling in English at school, she went on to receive an undergraduate degree in Philosophy and English Literature. In 2015, she founded and ran *The New Frontier* university magazine and became a published poet. She founded Softwood Self-Publishing two years later, where she now works with authors from across the world, editing a variety of manuscripts. The first of her novels in *The Dwelling Hunter* series was published in 2020.